SCF

FREDE

PREFACE

High into the north of England lies Newcastle-upon-Tyne, where one

rainy, wintry season I sat in the smoking area of a pub called Gunner Tavern. An obviously homeless man approached me asking for money. I gave what change I had and unwittingly purchased a conversation with the loose shrapnel from my pocket. I cannot remember his name but I do remember the things he said. He explained how hard it was, how hungry, disrespected and exhausted he was all the time.
What struck me most was his eloquent articulation and the way in which he described addiction. He said it was like having indigestion, how sometimes it makes you feel nauseous and sometimes it churns your guts until it's painful not to shit (I said he was eloquent, not elegant).
He was surprisingly not from Newcastle, as his accent sounded more from London, and I saw him often around Pink Lane and Westmorland Road - I was renting a studio flat I couldn't afford for my Master's degree in Creative Writing.
When I wasn't drinking in pubs I was working in one called The Forth Hotel and the homeless man often passed by its large windows and caught my eye. I wouldn't describe him as a friend as I'm sure he gave the same treatment to others in the area, but he was friendly enough.
His description of addiction somehow melded with my unhealthy obsession with Anglo-Saxon poetry (notably Beowulf) and soon was birthed the concept of my *Sceadugenga*, my palimpsest to one of the finest and earliest renditions of English literature.
You see, what may appear on its surface as a challenging, experimental and avant-garde book about the monster Grendel and all the Germanic mythos that pertains to him, actually began as an allegory for drug-addiction as described to me by this man, who I hope is still alive and well.
Amidst the veil of experimentalism, Old English, the avant-garde and all else in this piece of work (and I do mean "a piece of work") is its original true meaning, which I tell to you now in its half-form. To some authors their books are to be planned and executed like the building of a house; from blueprint to builder it is the same.
I am not capable of such a thing and instead plant a seed. I can always speculate as to the shape of the tree I plan to grow from its species, nature, variant or genome but ultimately each tree is unique and out of my control. The same goes for my approach to fiction.
I hope you do not suffer in reading this book as I suffered in writing it. It was not intended for pleasure but for remembrance...

Blēd þū mid þǣm sceadugengan, nā tō andgyte him, ac tō gemynde...
May you bleed with the Sceadugenga, not to understand him, but to

SCEADUGENGA

remember him...

INTRODUCTION

There is no path forward in Sceadugenga, pronounced "SHAH-doo-yen-ga". The plot, the protagonist and the motion of this story retreat back on themselves and through the mind of the inhuman. Please see Glossary at the back of this text for translations, pronunciations and other contexts.

Sometime in the first millennium A.D., in accordance with the Anglo-Saxon scripture, a man named Beowulf savagely tore the arm from the beast called Grendel, kindred to Cain and born of fen-lairs. If the tales are to be believed, poor, miserable, forlorn Grendel retreated to his home and promptly died.

One of the finest retellings of that epic poem is the novel *Grendel* (1971) by John Gardner. Second only to the source material, it is one of the highest inspirations to this novel (or "novella" if you prefer). Gardner proposed sympathy or at least empathy for Grendel, a decision which invokes Milton's *Paradise Lost* (1667), of which Blake said Milton was 'of the Devil's party without knowing it.' A more contemporary rendition of this concept is the song *Sympathy for the Devil* by the British rock band, The Rolling Stones. As readers we are often tempted to pity demons and villains; Dracula, Frankenstein's Monster and Mr. Hyde are all fantastic examples and inspirations for Sceadugenga. We need champions for our voyeuristic desires. Grendel surely meets the necessary criteria for this: he has a mother; he has a home; he feels deeply and even profoundly; he dies in pain; he suffers like a man might. In fact, it is Beowulf who is infallible, even godly. The eponymous hero dies only in old age whilst fighting a dragon, having achieved a noble stewardship of his kingdom, and cultivating fame in his questing youth. How could any of us relate to this?

Sceadugenga is a story which is aware of its contemporaries and predecessors. However, conceptually it is unique. The writing is comprised of three major registers — those being modern, syntactical English to reflect the modernity in Grendel, sentence fragments in moments of bloodthirsty hysteria, and Old English when the protagonist is... feeding shall we say. No matter which register dominates any particular section, any given extract is difficult to follow, and this is by design. The story is written so arrestingly within the eyes of the incomprehensible that many a reader may fail to realise what is happening for quite some time. Fortunately, a footnoted glossary and this introduction should ease the burden of understanding for even the most attentive of readers.

The chapters go backward in time (please consider omitting this paragraph to avoid any "spoilers"). The first is in the 2000s in Newcastle. The second is Belfast in the 70s. Then the third and fourth chapters are in London in the 1910s and 1880s respectively. The fifth takes a large leap to the Bastille during the French Revolution followed by Calais in the 1550s when it was taken back by the French from the English. The seventh chapter experiences the Black Plague in Cologne (1349). Another leap shows us chapters eight and nine, both finally reaching the time and place of *Beowulf* when Grendel's arm is torn off. To avoid a simple perspective retelling akin to Gardner's, the story takes many creative liberties and embellishments. The final chapter is in the present day in the Highlands, indicating the opening is an "in medias res". If the reader were to zoom out, they would see, plotted chapter by chapter, the looping, northward journey of Grendel in the millennia following his supposed death.

CHAPTER 1
Newcastle-upon-Tyne
2001

The seagulls don't sleep.
    Pink Lane is a stone's throw from Central Station. It's a small street, once known for its debauchery. A pink bakery now stands at its foot. No blood or semen remain on the pavement. Around the narrow corner of Fourth Lane is a remnant of its past: a massage parlour. Toothless men say that one can find a happy ending there.

The ruins of a black chimney are scattered on cobbles, surrounded by mizzle and shimmering in moonlight. A recent windstorm toppled it and fences have been put up, but pushed aside by drunkards. They won't let it obstruct their journey to the pub.

Whispering the sight of it: *'Eald enta geweorc.'*

The translation: ancient work of giants, from one language into itself, only in the future. Five drunk men stumble in loose formation. Sanctuary can be found in the shadow of Gunner Tavern, once called Gotham Town, infamously a shithole. Rolling a cigarette deters drunks, an excuse to keep eyes down, keep out of their business. It's always hard to roll a cigarette with only one hand, hard but worth it.

The plan works twofold: the men pass by and there's the cigarette to smoke as reward. Kiss the tip into the flame, stir it to life. Tendrils catch moonlight.

Sceadugenga is Shadow-Stalker or Walker-in-the-Night. Nightwalker maybe? Nightwalker... it's difficult to remember. Not all night is shadows as without the moon there are no shadows, only eventide.

Sceadugenga. Ic wille flæsc—

Flesh—

The Town Wall, closing for the night. Bartenders staying for a drink. A lock-in. Locked in with masoned stone, birdshit lampposts and beer kegs, empty and piled on each other. "Camden Town Brewery". "Hacher Pschorr München". "Fyne Ales". "Non-refundable 9g. Ratatonic abv 5.0%". Next to black bins. "Glass only — No food".

Līðs— calm.

A crooked grate tries to swallow a greasy deli bag. A cobbled gutter sucks in rain. The stream runs outside TL Multimedia Registered Office, collecting cigarette butts and a can of Red Bull. It ebbs by a puddle like a sluice to a sea. A graffiti-smiley-face watches on. It's crying in the drizzle.

The cobbles lead to Newcastle Central Station.

A telephone box is hardly visible under spray paint. It stands sentry in front of the station. Even so late, a flow of people move under the classical arches. A stumbling man pisses against a pillar. It's a hundred times larger than him but he misses all the same. He almost falls to the floor but a shadow of sobriety catches him.

The stabbing scent of rain on the tongue mingles with salami from a Subway. Hospital lights flicker over a meat counter and phlegm-green uniforms tremble together. The smudged silhouettes move through mizzled windows.

Another man keels over and retches just outside The Victoria Comet. Bile and beer spread over the pavement.

'I'm no-t dr-unk!'

The bouncer won't listen.

The cigarette is wet; it's given to the gutter.

The station is opposite to Basil Hume, or at least his bronze likeness. He has a hooked nose and large ears. By day it is an approachable face but by the night, his metallic wrinkles catch shadows. His metallic hair is unsoaked by downpour. His metallic eyes are slick with rain that looks like tears. Even with an arm outstretched and a palm turned open, he looked like a shadowy monster.

A rock is behind him, waist-high with an Old English inscription. It's too dark to read, let alone translate. *Almigtig* is all that's visible.

'Almighty.'

The writing is covered in moss, clumping and draping. It drinks the rain. Its colour shows from light across the two-lane road: Neville Street turning into the A186. The light is from a supermarket hidden in the classical building.

The gutter has turned from cobble into cut marble. It follows the road and leads away from the statue.

"Other Routes" to the left or "P Central Station Short Stay" to the right. A car in the wrong lane signals for "Other Routes". A truck won't let it in. Neither budges. Their horns blare but the truck's is louder. The car accepts its fate.

Up ahead is a blue horizon. Not blue of the sky. Not blue of the sea. Not blue that belongs.

A lab coat moves in a window, cranes over a microscope. The white of the room, several levels up, looks sterile. An empty bottle of Buckfast tonic wine rolls down the pavement. 'Stop Cancer' shines on a bus-stop where a nurse sleeps on the bench.

'Can I talk to you, pal?' A slurred voice. It comes from nowhere, a wispy beard and vacant face, with eyes that see right through you — eyes brighter than the statue's.

'*Nō.*'

'No worries, have-a-good-night-then.' The words string together. It wouldn't be the first time they were said that night, and definitely not the last.

Black, yellow-topped bollards stand beneath the NHS Centre's entrance. Above, a blue "L", a green "i", a red and italicised "*f*" and an orange "e". Within is a square with lines of people queuing under neon. "Rusty's" has a cashpoint next to it then "Disco Junkyard" and "Digital". The people are bright and colourful. They vibrate warmth and blood but quiver anyway.

Opposite stand naked trees and "Biomedicine West Wing". "Science Centre Entrance". Eight one-litre bottles of water line a windowsill up on high. They catch the blinking light of an activated security system.

There's a brick-stone building in the centre of the square, a blue circle on its side. "John Dobson designed this market keeper's office and toll house in 1831".

Dried gum sticks to the floor in the hundreds, maybe thousands. They've been there so long they become one with the stone, flat and hardened in time.

'Alright, pet?' The voice is from the queue, drunk and inquisitive, bored even. She's at the end of the line. 'What's wrong with your arm?'

She wears rolled curls and heels that could run you through, and tangerine-tinted skin. She blinks bright eyes, ringed with blackness. Sooted lids, heavy lids brush the wind.

Behind is "Cafe Shop Entrance". The entrance is the exit to Times Square.

"Heineken" is sandwiched between Scotswood Road and Churchill Street. They're anchored by pubs, but beyond is Safestore Self Storage, an ever-glowing yellow sign in industrial plots. "50% off for up to 8 weeks". "We sell boxes and packaging".

There's a triangular warning sign, the roadworks symbol that looks like a man struggling with an umbrella. It's weighed down by a rotting sandbag.

Microbreweries are hidden from the mizzle, stinging neon under a railway bridge. "Mosaic Tap" is quite popular. The muffled thud of music comes from the brewery, and behind the fogged windows there's movement. "Crowne Plaza" shimmers in the distance. It's high up and breaks through the mizzle: a purple beacon.

Low Bridge Ahead — 4.6m or 15'3". Corrugated iron rungs vibrate above and drip water. Black tarmac groans under the weight of vans and lorries that are lower than 4.6m or 15'3". The walls flake brown brick. They glow red with brake-lights and the sound of the road and cars grows in the echo. Three men with cans of Stella Artois move to single formation on the narrow pavement to pass. Torsos turn askew in the loud tunnel and a queue of vehicles builds up. One Volkswagen Golf doesn't notice and hits the back of an Audi. It sounds like something breaks but no marks are to be seen. The red-lined silhouette of the man puts his head in his hands. Both pull up outside the tunnel and get out, exchange information.

There's a 3-way intersection marked by the tunnel, "Northumbria Police" with a chequered sign and "Sachins finest Punjabi cuisine". The Punjabi restaurant is a Byzantine building, embroidered with blue and white. To the right, as the road goes down a hill, red-brick neo-classical architecture. The buildings get taller, or the road gets lower. "Caviar Studios". There are few cars and fewer people. The slope levels out. Out here the city is thinning, darkening.

A high up, suspended and unnamed railway bridge appears from the mizzle. There are no lights on it until a train goes through. The rattling of it scatters through the dark. The bridge's silhouette sheds a lining of dew as it rumbles. The train and its lit windows trundle into town, the bridge once again invisible. A reverberating tremor sounds until it doesn't. Right underneath where it was, there's no indication it exists anymore, except for the occasional drip from still-wet iron bolts.

The drip falls into a damp carpark. Cars, pushed against bracken, huddle together, no movement in any window. It's hard to say if the carpark is abandoned or not, with cars but no people. Empty, they hold no flesh. *Flæsc.*

Muþa, the mouth of a river, but also a door or an opening. If the water goes out to sea, it's spewing quietly. If it goes inland, upstream, it inhales the sea, the *mere*. It's quiet. Its surface doesn't have ripples; it has only subtle imperfections that catch the light, rashes of streetlight taken by the tide.

They say the Tyne was once a cradle for ships during the Empire, but it can't have been more impressive than the Thames in the 1880s. The sounds and smell was enough to go by.

Flæsc— Flæsc—

The river's empty. Quiet bracken banks and roads running

alongside. Adjacent road is called Close. Cycle Route 72 in between.

"Acquisition Aesthetics - Botox and Dermal Filler Courses Provider", hidden down by the river. "Copthorne Hotel - 4 star hotel" or "Travel Lodge - 2 star hotel". Both are empty.

Flæsc—
Flesh—
Across the river is another carpark. Mizzle-haloes around streetlights. The light glimmers off the slicked cars. They're sleeping in the rain.

A building across the Tyne. One level, not even that. Red brick, tiled roof, blue-coloured railing. Composite fences as high as the building. A light shows graffiti on its side. A sign describing what it's for, sticking out of the roof with tiles. On the other side of the river it's impossible to see what it says. There's the light. It has a halo of rain. Light only shows the graffiti. "OTRAS", written bulbous and overlapping. Mizzle-haloes.

Lið s— calm.

A man stands on the opposite the bank of the Tyne, setting up fishing rods, each tipped with a different-coloured light. He has a knitted cap and a handlebar moustache, calloused hand-flesh. He hobbles from putting up a fishing rod and sits on a bench opposite. He has six fish. The largest one is in the middle. Their eyes are open and stare out as if they're still alive. Their mouths are open like they're surprised. They're shiny in the streetlamps and mizzle. Fins drip with rainwater. Scales shimmer in moonlight.

The river is the same. It doesn't change and it never will.

A large sandstone building stands, red-tiled roof and windows painted white. The bulk of the building is smooth, surrounded with scaffolding entwined with fairy lights. On a table there's a "Coors Light" pint glass filling with rain and a green "Peroni" bottle as its empty companion. There's a blue and white striped straw dissolving in the damp, merging with the surface of the table. An old beer barrel looks out of place, with rusted rungs and wilted flowers on top, so wilted they can't soak the air's moisture. All is left unattended, but the inside of the pub is busy. Glassy apertures are fogged. A bottle of vinegar's smudged outline is moved from the inside of a windowsill to be dribbled onto someone's fish and chips. The sound of many people speaking comes from the door when a woman leaves through the front.

It sounds like *Heorot*, the Hall long forgotten, home of the arm-above-the-throne. There are even fires burning inside the pub. It looks and sounds so similar, a thousand years later. Except... no warriors— *nāne Scyldingas*, no one to defend the hall. A herd, a herd of—

Heord of flæsc.
Flæsc—
"THE QUAYSIDE." "Food Served All Day." "Award - Winning Wines." "lavAzza coffee." "Global Beers." "Cask Ales." "World - Class Spirits." A white symbol of a person in a wheelchair. "Assistant Dogs Only."

"No drinks are permitted outside of the beer garden or customers standing on the outside of the walled perimeter. Thank you."

The inside is filled with voices. It has no smell but the nose is filled somehow. *Flæscbræp—* flesh-scent. Geordie voices compete over each other. Two men clink their 'Stella Artois' goblets together. They spill froth onto the table. *Béordruncen*. Beer-drunk.

The bar is long with many taps and logos:
"Corona Extra." "Strongbow Dark Fruit Cider." "Stella Artois." "Carling." "Leffe Blonde." "Coors cold as the rockies." "Bud Light." "Carlsberg Danish Pilsner." "Stowford Press Apple Cider." "Shipyard EST. Portland Maryland USA, American Pale Ale, Refreshing, Citrus, Full Flavour." "Budweiser." "Strongbow." "Stella Artois."

On the other end of the bar:
"Leffe Blonde." "Guinness. Super Chilled." "Stella Artois." "Kopparberg Strawberry & Lime." "San Miguel Especial." "Worthington's Creamflow." "Stella Artois." "Brewdog Punk IPA." "Bud Light." "Corona Extra." "Carling." "Coors cold as the rockies." "Budweiser."

Líðs— calm.

Black beams make the building look old-fashioned. The people do as well. Anoraks and umbrellas shake off the rain. They gather around the bar. There are six bartenders. Most are young men and women with an older manager. He is the only one with a collared shirt on. He stands, looks and watches and they serve.

Above the Quayside Wetherspoons the High Level Bridge glows with its streetlights. People walk along it, their shadows the only indication they're there. The bridge is beige. A train goes over its top and a car drives through. The first bridge with both railway and motorcar infrastructure in the world, or so the locals say. It looks like something from the mid-1800s. After enough time, one can determine the different ages of corrugated metal— something in the way they shine and glisten in mizzle. There was so much metal down south, hauled around, making more noise than the trains of the High Level Bridge could ever.

Underneath the bridge there is a restaurant called "House of

Tides." The lights are off. It has a sign like a pub, overhanging and loose. It drips water. The sound is both rhythmic and irregular.

The droplets splat into a carpark like before, only this time from higher up. The sound spooks the silhouette of a rat. It squeaks and scurries across the tarmac. It draws near, but seeing its mistake, widens the whites of its eyes and reels in dread. Prey.

Rætt— flæsc— flæsc—

Cars parked underneath the High Level Bridge. Tesla - MD21 STA. Audi - BL71 STA. Fiat - RN11 SOA. Highway Maintenance Van - ND19 SBA. Fiat - WT03 SOA. Grey Mercedes - CLA SSA. Blue Mercedes - GP23 SOA. *Niðnihtlicgeweorc*. A naked tree.

Metal fences in the carpark up against the Wetherspoons. Holds in *dræst—*

No— rubbish, waste.

Lið́s.

They hold in waste that is cardboard and wood. They've been shunted aside like the fences around the fallen chimney of Pink Lane. Except they're slanted on the mossy ground. The moss drinks the rain and there is no slickness. The moss is the gutter. They're like church lichens. *Ciricragu*, except they're still alive and don't cling to gravestones. They only cling to cobbles underneath dripping bridges with people and trains and cars and trucks.

The stairs, *bēoþ forþgānde wið sćeadwum—*

The stairs are going up into shadows.

It's next to the House of Tide. Stone slabs ascend unevenly, held in place by narrow brick walls, graffiti on both sides. The stairway is well lit towards its base, but quickly darkens and the top is shadow.

There are boarded up windows and doors running up alongside the stairs.

Flæsc—

White graffiti. Most of it can't be read. "FAD" is one. A splatter of blue paint. Symbols mixed with letters of indeterminate meaning. They might have meant something to the vandal, but dried up, they flake underneath streetlight saying nothing. There's a signature in black writing. Three large white arrows coming from the ground, from a corner of the threshold that looks urine-stained.

Meaningless *tácn—*

Symbols. Meaningless symbols.

Bits of a black broken bottle scatter on the steps. A clay air vent drips with something, crumbling at the edges. On the right of the stairwell, bushes hang over with small weeds and large, naked stems.

They overhang a metal door with many colours of different graffiti, none of it on the brick walls.

The stairs plunge into shadow at the top. Almost half is in darkness.

Sćeadwum— shadows.

A carpark at the top. "PRIVATE T/BULL" written twice in double yellow lines. To the right, "WARNING", "priority police response". "Monitored by CCTV' pushed up against a metal fence. It stands upright this time, but some of its wires are bent and pulled askew.

Further from the carpark, a large brick tunnel with double yellow lines on either side of the tarmac. A large crack in the road. Bicycle bars. The bridge is made of large bricks. Some of them are chalky. Some of them are beige and sandy. Some of them are grey. All of them are wet. Still raining mizzle.

A rain-shower.

Regnscur—

"This bridge is LEN3/325 — Queen Lane, Newcastle." "In the event of any vehicle striking this bridge please phone THE RAILWAY AUTHORITY on 01904 71804 as quickly as possible. The safety of the trains could be affected." No train sounds come from the top of the bridge.

Lið s— calm.

On its other side, the pavement splits open in places like a puddle. It shows cobbles underneath with some dried wads of gum. Another railway can be seen a stone's throw from the first one, topped with a metallic enforcement structure and metal railings. Bollards look like the teeth of another tunnel, hungry teeth of a stone maw. This tunnel is made of corrugated iron that glows orange with upwards-facing lights. To its right is the Newcastle Castle. It's tall and made of pale stones. An old set of rusted iron bars at its base. A few of the glazed arrow slits are lit by modern lamps, unfit for old stone. Most of them are dark, but shimmer in slickness. A streetlight is up against the castle. It has a halo of mizzle around it.

A line of cars gathers outside *se burg*—

Castle. It's a castle.

A line of cars gathers outside the castle.

They wait at the at the end of the tunnel. The brake-lights mix with the orange, upwards-facing lights on the corrugated iron. It rumbles with a train, sheds droplets from bolts. They splat on the roofs of the cars. There's a mist of rain in the tunnel.

To the right of the cars is the Black Gate. Most of its lights are on. The windows look newer than the arrow-slits and battlements of the

Newcastle Castle. It's surrounded by a dried-out moat. A couple stands underneath the bridge that runs through the gate. They're kissing in the streetlight. Pushed together they look like one wider person. One of them leans away and laughs. Then the other pulls them together again. They kiss once more. There's an umbrella lying on the floor next to them. It's still open. Hateful... *Laþlic— Laþlic—*

Ða com of more under sceadumisthleoþum... me. The couple pick up their umbrella and walk out into the mizzle. They're holding hands.

Sceadugenga—

They walk huddling under the umbrella.

Sceadugenga—

'Oi, pal.' A rough voice. It's weak, echoed from an alcove under the bridge next to the Black Gate. It's not clear where exactly the voice came from, then a lighter strikes and a cigarette is lit. "Oi, pal!" A homeless man, huddled inside one of the archways of the bridge. He's smoking a cigarette. The archway-alcove looks disused. It was definitely used for something centuries ago. The memory of what it was has faded. It serves a new purpose now.

There are warped stones in the centre. It smells of rat shit, a musty and earthy scent. One corner of the alcove's threshold has a burst gutter above it. It's been leaking for so long down the stone-brick that it looks like a riverbed, mossed and sludged with slickness.

The entrance looks like mire-land. It looks like home, the smell of green pungency and slime. The slurry of shining stone and mizzle resembles a bygone time, like a fen-lair that's gone.

It's dry inside the alcove. The rain does not reach inside. The cigarette moves from illuminating one face, old and wrinkled, to another, young and hollow. The young-and-hollow man takes a drag, then passes it further through *se sćeadwum*. The third man who receives it is middle-aged with a beard that looks dry. His skin is flaking off and his eyes are almost impossible to see between his bulbous eyebrow and cheekbone.

Sceadugenga—

'Mate.' The first looks older with his grey hair, which is only visible when the cigarette is passed back to him. 'Do you have a snout? This is our last one.'

He accepts the cigarette packet given to him.

'Are you sure, pal? Thanks a lot. Christ, where's your arm? Look lads...'

His eyes light up with a new cigarette, watching the stranger, the *Sceadugenga*.

The cigarette glows orange and crackles, showing liver spots on his temples and no teeth in his mouth. His face looks rounded at the corners. He swallows his own chin. He swallows his own flesh—

Flæsc—

The young man looks warily at the newcomer. His eyes think something is wrong. He twitches and blinks. The middle-aged man seems steady, not shaking or twitching. He picks at his knuckles. His dark beard-hairs shimmer with the inhalation of the cigarette. The three begin to fill the alcove with smoke. The smoke billows outside, swallowed by mizzle.

"What's your name?" the young-and-hollow man asks. He still looks wary.

Flæsc—

He receives no answer. He'll know, though.

Flæsc—

There's no one nearby. The alcoves are a quiet part of a busy city centre.

They're very quiet.

Rumbles with distant trains.

Ic bíte into flæsc. Ic āþeġe. Ic ásúge þá steorfan, min hungor bierneð, gelíc eoten bealuhygdig. Heira drēora, þára drēora bestīemað mín tungan. Se ealdurnan ācwyle fyrst. He cennð bānum und pīnnessum, se cnafa āscað mé arian.

He onginð befleon swá sum nēatum butan sum adelsceaþe. He biergð better ac hit is ne genyhtsum. Se þridda mann costað beorgan his orfeorme frēondum ac he mæg ne be mé. Anbyrdnes? Gōd.

Ic feohte und he feohteð. Ic locie eat fyr his frēondum ac he is a mene wésa. Gōd. Regn gelic blōde, ge blod gelic regne. Regnscur. Blodscur. Ic undýde hine, bestīeme hine in him selfum.

Liðs—

✸ ✸ ✸

The alcove is now disused again. The burst gutter leaks water and mossy sludge. They trickle down into puddles of still-warm blood which mingles to a pink liquid. The middle-aged man's hand twitches death throes in the archway's threshold. A small pool gathers in his palm which spasms. The hands of the old and wrinkled man are very still in the shadows. The young-and-hollow man lies folded over a waist-high rock. All their dead eyes are slick with either rain or tears; they look metallic and a train rumbles metallic in the distance.

Out into the mizzle, *se sceadugenga.*

CHAPTER 2
Belfast
1972

The streets are heavier at night.
The weight and smell of rain can't wash itself off the tarmac.
The road snakes up with glowing streetlights to a large hill. It's hard to see it at night, except for its large black swelling which blots out the pale clouds of the horizon. It looks like a tumour in the ground, the hill. Perhaps the houses gathering at its base are symptoms. Maybe pus.
The houses all look the same along Cavehill Road. It's a long street. There aren't many shops or restaurants, so there aren't many people walking at night.
Except *se sceadugenga*.
The houses are all the same shape. They line up in the hundreds. The only thing differentiating them from one another is the colour or paintwork. Some are redbrick; some are redbrick painted white; some are redbrick painted grey. The houses on Cavehill look like the cars parked: all the same shape with different colours.
Líðs— Líðs—
There aren't many people around in the evenings. The wind stirs and picks some leaves, swirls them about in the middle of the road. The leaves disperse when a black car drives through them. It moves in the direction of the hill at the end of the road. It's brake-lights make haloes of red around themselves. They look like bloodthirsty eyes.
Líðs—
A fire station at an intersection has a light on on its first floor. The shaded shape of a man in uniform sits over a phone. He rocks gently back and forth and puffs on the silhouette of a cigarette. Good idea.
A few fingers grip the rolling paper while the tobacco rests in the palm... rolling cigarettes with one hand is impossible.
Ācyrsa þone Gēat...
Eventually it's rolled. Kiss the cigarette tip into the flame, stir it to life.
It smokes well; the dry night lets the little glow crackle softly, undisturbed.
A young couple walks slowly down the other side of the

pavement. The other side of the road has less light, a better place to avoid others. The couple walks by while laughing about something.

Laþlic—

There are always couples, no matter which city or decade.

The road snakes on for a while, a good place to walk. There are large trees in between every other lamppost. They make long shadows over cars and house birds which shit on them. The trees all look the same, well-groomed into nearly spherical, nearly conical shapes like bushes stabbed into poles.

The houses begin to become more spaced out closer to the hill. They become a bit more blocky. A small green service-box has red graffiti on it and wisteria drowning it. It looks like a *rætt—*

It looks like a rat caught in a net.

The wisteria grows from a building that's larger than the rest. It's redbrick like all the others but its symmetrical and has blue signs saying, "ENTRANCE".

Behind it there's a green stretching out to Sunningdale Park, just opposite Tivoli Gardens. Steely tendrils of smoke coil through the still night air. The street is long and maybe a hundred steps have been taken, but the hill beyond still looks the same size, the same blotting out of stars.

Lióðs—

Everything is calm now. Not many people wander the street. The weather is mild. The clouds seem locked in place with the absence of wind and no birds make any sounds. The streetlights glow constantly. One further down the road flickers spasmodically every few seconds. It blinks and flutters its light, making a momentary halo around itself before snuffing out for a moment, and doing it all again.

Its been flickering from when the sun set over the houses' pointed roofs to now, just a few hours after a nearby church chimes midnight. Near to the flickering streetlight is a redbrick house with lace curtains drawn shut, but the windows are cracked open. The muffled sound of metallic voices comes from the window, and the faint silhouette of a hunched over person moves. It's too hard to resist.

Closer to the cracked open window, the metallic voices sound like their coming from a radio. The hunched over silhouette turns the volume up and adjusts the signal. It makes the sound of scratchy static like a dying rat.

'...and reports are still coming in about the mass shooting in Ballymurphy. With twelve now confirmed dead, tensions in Catholic districts and elsewhere in Belfast and Derry seem to be only rising. We have a statement from a member of the congregation of Father Hugh

Mullan, a thirty eight year old priest shot whilst attempting to aid the wounded. Hello, madam. Thanks for joining us...'

The radio is turned down by another silhouette who enters from the side. It's hard to tell through the laced curtains which are drawn shut, but they appear to be an old man and woman. The light comes from a lamp in the corner of the room and a black picture is raised above the radio. Beneath it is a crucifix. It seems to look out from its perch, a vigilant watchman.

Sceadugenga bið þrēatod—

There are many Christian symbols in the city, many churches which can't be stepped near.

Laþlic—

Líðs—

Breathing in the cigarette is calming.

'What're you doing up?'

'I couldn't sleep. It's just so awful.'

'I know but you can't listen to round-the-clock stations in the middle of the night, Mary. Life goes on. We have to get on with our days and not let fear-mongering control our nights.'

'That's easy for you to say. You never have trouble sleeping.'

'To be fair. Let me make you a cup of tea. It'll fix you right— have you been smoking?'

'I never!'

The male figure begins to move to the window. The cigarette is tossed in the bushes.

The other side of the road is darker this time. It's better to walk through. The swelling beyond Cavehill Road looks onwards, a blackness on the horizon.

The sound of the window closing comes from behind. The streetlight starts flickering again. Closer to it, there's the sound of the glitching bulbs like blood-flow made of fire, sputtering. It keeps going. It keeps flickering. It's the only one on the street which stretches on for a mile in each direction. In other cities, a long street might be wider, have more lanes and no parked cars. But on Cavehill Road there were cars parked face-to-face from beginning to end and little deviation in the width of the road. It looked like an ordinary residential road with its nearly-spherical, nearly conical trees and dim streetlights.

Cavehill Road, probably named for its alignment to the hill in the distance, looks nearly unremarkable except for its length, like a purgatory of nearly suburban homes and cars.

Se sceadugenga— walks alone down Cavehill Road.

Belfast is a lonelier place than all the others. But solitude is safer.

Loneliness is safe.

The place where an arm used to be begins to ache, pretends to be still be there.

Fals earm— if only the Doctor were still around to help.

But loneliness is safe.

Cavehill Road stretches on, but the hill draws closer. The swelling looms.

Still no one in the street since the couple walked by. Soon the trees begin to feel like company, but they don't even rustle. The night is so still.

Cooldarragh Park is to the left and a give-way line almost faded out. Henderson Avenue is to the right and it forks off at a forty-five degree angle. It's even narrower than Cavehill Road and stretches off in the distance in an unbroken line.

The streets in the city are lonely and long. The people don't walk them at night.

It's *líðs*— but it's very lonely.

A collection of small, one-storey shops cluster on the left beyond the turning to Henderson Avenue. They line up and face the road. They look so odd in the middle of endless houses. They break the monotony. There's a "Fruit Store" next to "Select Food Store Lt."

There's a ladies hair stylist called "Marguerite" and a "Benson & Hedges, Confectioner, H.Y. Boden, Fancy Goods". They're all shut up for the night and quiet, but out of place in the length of Cavehill Road's endlessness. Even though the shops are all different in name and font, they're the same cuboid shape neatly lined up next to one another like a designated shopping centre. These small shops must entertain the whole street. There's little else along its two miles of length.

A dark car with its headlights off pulls up slowly down the road. Its slinking like a crouched animal, like a wolf in a fen-lair that's spotted prey. It drives quietly and slowly in between the two snaking lines of parked cars. The shadow of a tree in a good place to watch and avoid being seen. The smell of diesel spreads behind it, a sickly, belched odour.

The car pulls to a stop outside the shopping centre.

Nā, ic eom gesewen—

The car must have stopped because it saw something... someone.

Líðs— perhaps it didn't.

The car doesn't move. Its lights are still off. Maybe they don't work.

The dark car adjusts its wheels and parallel parks in front of the shops. It stays still for several minutes with its engine running. The exhaust pipe has an old muffler which trembles and shoots out a small cloud of fumes which dissipate quickly in the mild night air. The car sits for a while longer.

The passenger door opens and then the driver's door. Two men step out, both with caps on and their collars turned up. They look up and down Cavehill Road, even at the shadows on the trees in between the glow of the streetlights. They see nothing

Se sceadugenga stands well within the shadow.

The men walk quickly down the street in the opposite direction to the dark hill, perhaps towards the city's centre. They keep their hats turned low and occasionally look over their shoulders. They walk and walk, never breaking stride and never failing to check over their shoulder. They'd be good prey, good *flæsc*—

Líðs—

No need. A few more decades of abstinence would be needed. There are too many people in cities.

Líðs—

Before long the two men were no more than small shifting shapes nearly a mile down Cavehill Road. None would know they were moving there if they hadn't seen them earlier. The car sits quietly in front of the shops.

There's another small green service-box to the right. It has illegible graffiti on it.

Towards the end of Cavehill Road the houses begin to thin out. It feels more like suburbia and fewer cars have parked this far down the street. Perhaps the free parking spot would not have been worth the long drive.

It's pleasant at night, though. The air is mild and the hill looms ever closer. Maybe its colder than most nights. It doesn't look like there's any wind on the hill. Even with gentle breezes and on pale nights, wind shows on the grassy faces of hills in the distance. They often sweep through and turn the blades of grass to make fleeting streaks of silvery ribbons dashing across the inclined meadow. It often looks like ripples catching moonlight on water's surface.

But no such thing shows on the face of the hill. It only looks like a still, dead swelling, blotting out the pale-black sky beyond. If there were any stars out, their light would be swallowed by the hill into its darkness. The mass looms closer.

Cavehill Road begins to come to an end. The already thinning-out houses begin to become so infrequent that it doesn't qualify for a street anymore.

Cutting across into a wide intersection is North Circular Road. It seems more deserving of being a long road. It's breadth puts Cavehill to shame.

Across the intersection, for no cars were driving that night, is Upper Cavehill Road.

Endeþ hit næfre—

Does it never end?

Upper Cavehill Road looks like Cavehill Road only with more fences and slightly larger houses. Apart from that, there are the redbrick walls, the nearly spherical, nearly conical trees dispersed between the dim streetlights.

Further up, some of the trees begin to match the houses and become larger. Some houses have gardens with their own trees. A cherry tree overhangs the pavement and opposite a young holm oak pokes its top over a fence.

That was a bad idea from the gardener. Holm oaks can too grow big with broad roots. The name sounds familiar.

Holm—

Holly.

The holly oak. It makes sense given the leaves look like they belong on a holly tree.

Looking up to the hill there are no trees to be seen. Nothing dares grow on the summit of the barren thing except grass, which in the summer heat looks dried out and tired. Around its base is a cluster of trees, not enough to be a forest, but dense enough to be considered together, a company.

The sound of a dog barking breaks the silence of the night. It's close by and smells something it doesn't like.

Maybe a rat. Maybe *se sceadugenga—*

Quicken to the hill. Dogs can break their chains and streets can be awoken.

The street loses its pavements and slopes upwards to the hill. The houses on the right are no longer there and soon the last house is passed. Behind, the flat city of Belfast stretches out into itself. The city glows a gentle hue and twinkles as if the stars are plucked from the pale, cloudy night sky and dropped on the small houses.

"Welcome to Cavehill Country Park" says a sign by a gate. The small black gate is propped up by two stone-stacked pillars. They look strong but the gate looks weak.

The path beyond it extends shrubs and then into a kind of dingle. Its louder in the trees and the shrubs. Animals are making noise.

The bark of foxes sound against one another and birds signal which branch they choose to sleep in. Even a deer sounds in the distance.

Flæsc—

No. There would be no catching it.

Líðs—

The shade of the trees break for a bit and a small sea of still ferns stretch out in a clearing. Only when emerging from the cover of trees is the sound of the city heard. When walking its streets, its silent. But from afar, the constant and subtly distant drone of stone and steel and glass and rubber and smoke stretches its finger out in all directions.

There's not much to do but inspect the top of the hill. Perhaps shelter can be taken in the woods when the sun rises. Then again, it looks like there's might be too much traffic on the footpath. Maybe deeper in would be better.

Some pine trees rise up in front of the path.

A sign says "Belfast Castle", "The White Stone" and "McArt's Fort".

Perhaps there are places to sleep in there.

The footpath right is completely shrouded in darkness and tree-shadow. It's easier to see in than daytime. The daytime is always blinding. The nighttime easier.

Further into the path, it feels accidental. Less like a manmade footpath and more like mistakenly trodden way through thick undergrowth and thickets. The path cuts through with deliberation, like it's trying to prove it's in charge and not the undergrowth — it's losing. The trees encroach over its top like a canopy. In the pale light their branches and leaves make dapple shadows on the muddy track.

Foxgloves are on the left. They waft in the wind. They're the only splash of colour aside from green and black and silvery black in any direction. They smell sweet. They smell sickly.

Bræþ—

No point in getting upset with flowers. They make no noise.

The animals make hooting or cawing or crooning sounds when *se sceadugenga* passes by. Most prey animals make that sound. The owls are silent. The badgers and foxes are silent. Once there were wolves which roamed around hills like this one. No longer.

Beech trees to the right as the slope begins to steepen. They don't look very old, the kind of trees which are still concerned with looking symmetrical, pretty. The older ones gnarl and twist with wisdom. There are few on the hill.

A bramble snags.

Wælhreowa—

It draws blood on a knuckle, a knuckle which has been wetted with its fair share of blood. It smells gangrened, putrid, foul. It's not the blood of prey. It catches the moonlight in the most peculiar way. The bramble isn't a manmade weapon, so it makes sense it can snag and draw blood. It's still enraging though.

Þæt bræmbor is ætstemped, afræst fram his wyrtrum—
The bramble is stamped out, ripped from its roots...

That dark, predatory blood has not been spilled for a long time. It reeks. It's *laþlic.*

Blackberries scatter over the muddy path and spill their juice. The little balls of their flesh stick to the mud and mingle. They smell sweet and sickly like the gardenia flowers.

Animals are watching the scene with curiosity. It's embarrassing. Only one set of knuckles and they manage to snag on brambles. The bramble is left behind, trampled into the mud and its own blackberries.

The path leads to a carpark. There are no cars in it. It's just a flat plateau of tarmac catching the night's light.

A good place to sleep.

Not good, but good as any. Amongst the trees, the animals would watch, and near the houses down at the bottom of the hill, the dogs would bark and the people would come and inspect. The people in charge of the trail at the hill must have closed it down for the night to stop people leaving their cars there. The carpark looks empty without them. It looks naked.

Lying in the middle, three limbs are spread-eagled and two eyes stare up at the pale clouds above. They don't move and look as if they're closer than they are.

The bright sky might prevent sleep, so maybe the trees would be a better idea. Perhaps a thick bush like a rhododendron or a holly would be wise, no need to wake up in time to move away from the cars and the brightness of the sun.

There's a nice holly bush with its splayed out leaves and a view through the trees of the city, which stretches out and twinkles. Good enough place to sleep.

Se sceadugenga slæpð—

※ ※ ※

A sky trembles. The air from the city shifts and judders. It's the middle of the day.

What is happening…
Hwæt cymþ—
Maybe he was found. Maybe they had come for him…
Ic eom gefunden! Hīe cōmon for mē—
The holly bush trembles. Something odd is happening, but it isn't happening nearby. It is in the city. The sound comes from below. There are the sounds of people murmuring about on the trail up to the top of the hill. Normally there would be no sense in leaving the holly bush until nightfall, but under the canopy of the thick trees away from the trail, the sun could not do its harm.

'Mother of God.' The voice of an older man speaks. His frame can be made out near the carpark, holding a young child to his chest. 'They've done it again. They're using the cars. Catharine, cover his eyes, will you.'

It makes no sense. What's happening…
Hwæt cymþ—
They're all looking down at the city.

Through the holly bush, away from the eyes of the sun and the eyes of the people. There's a better view of the city that way.

The city looks its usual self, only there's something different. Over a dozen plumes of smoke rise up like tendrils in the daylight. It's a bright day and the birds are making the kind of noises which people like. Only now there is the sound of countless sirens flashing through the city. They coalesce into a long droning sound which sounds, from the top of the barren hill, very similar to the air-raid sirens back in London. That was a strange sound and since, nothing has been able to recreate it, except for the imitation coming from the city below. The plumes are dark, too dark to be from deliberate fires. The smoke is of destruction.

One plume of smoke is very close. It's at the top of Cavehill Road. It's around where the car stopped the night before. The sight of police and ambulances and the sound of sirens and people shouting make their way up the hill and mingle with the trees and the leaves and the bushes and the mud.

'Oh, God.' It's a different voice from the trail. 'What do we do?'
'There's nothing we can do.'

They're right. People can rarely do anything. Then again, it's people that do the things which others are powerless to stop. People are odd. Other livestock doesn't act that way.

Not really.

CHAPTER 3
Battersea
1917

The city is growing.
Battersea is an unusual place. Its broad streets stretch along its southern side, and a park against the Thames.

Battersea Park Road is one of those broad streets. Wagons and trams once trundled along its length, cutting over the tracks. Not many disturb the street anymore. It's been quiet for a few years, and the nights go largely undisturbed - except for two years ago, when the Zeppelins came in.

They were magnificent. They cruised like North Sea whales, slowly migrating over London. Their swollen bodies blotted out the stars and large spears of light were thrown up, fiery metals exchanged in great numbers between the earth and sky.

Some bodies were left on the streets, perfect to be picked at by crows or other things. They were like carrion.

There is no one out on Battersea Park Road. Streetlamps glow brightly and show St. Saviour's Church, a detestable thing. It watches *se sceadugenga*, aware of everything. The Doctor has taught about the local area in great detail.

'Don't be afraid of churches,' he had said. What does he know?'

The church was built in 1870, with some masoned, Kentish ragstone for its face. It has dressed quoins and a dark, heavy roof of timber trusses with points around its chancel and knave. It points a steeple high into the sky, piercing the beautiful night with its putrid piety.

The church is left behind. Moving eastwards down Battersea Park Road, there are shops shut down for the night.

"Segalls For Value", "The Real Welsh Flannel House" has a broad sign curling around the flattened corner of the redbrick building, leading onto the Kilton Street. A stink pipe pretends to be a lamppost, slowly and almost silently spewing smoke from its mouth. Listening closely, the low hum of the hot air can be heard ringing through the thick, green metal.

The structures all look quiet in the night, not a soul disturbing them. sticks out from the line of buildings. A sound comes from a small byroad leading south in the direction of Clapham. The tramlines all coalesce down a street and down to Clapham Junction.

The shape of a soldier in uniform leans against a wall, streetlights leading south silhouetting him. He's steadying himself. He looks drunk. There's no one else around. The sound of a distant tram rattling and squeaking through the smog sounds. The soldier can hardly lift his head. Easy prey.

Flæsc—
Flesh—
No. The Doctor would never allow—
Flæsc—
"Spiers and Pond Laundry". "Funeral - Henry Smith." next to "W. Shaw & Son Picture House." "Freeman Hardy & Willis for Boots and Shoes - Branches Everywhere!"

Quickly to Macduff Road.

In the distance a bridge with a train. "Grosvenor Wine and Spirits." "BANK." "Stop."

Polytechnic Institute of Technology. Old car rusting.

"2 Macduff Road." "4 Macduff Road." "6 Macduff Road." "8 Macduff Road." "10 Macduff Road." "12 Macduff Road." "14 Macduff Road." "16 Macduff Road." "18 Macduff Road."

"20 Macduff Road."

Líðs—

The knocker is sounded.

The dark, wooden door to 20 Macduff Road swings open silently on its hinges, its hinges catching the soft glow of the small street. 20 Macduff Road is the end of the street. It's a corner house which looks Victorian, and was built in the 1870s.

It's darker than Battersea Park Road, as that street has arc lamps which are powered by the recent introduction of electricity in Battersea. Macduff Road has gas-powered lamps which are turned on by the lamplighter when the sun begins to set, which is relatively late in June. The church chimes distantly.

'Come in, you fool. Do you want to be seen lingering?'

It's the Doctor's voice. He's always very protective and insistent, despite his age. An old hand welcomes in, closing the door.

The inside of the house is warmer than outside. A gas lantern is lit by the Doctor. The white, phosphorescent glow stains his nearly blind eyes and deepens his wrinkles. The Doctor rarely speaks about his age but he looks somewhere over eighty now.

'Where did you go?'

He receives no answer.

Se sceadugenga gæð niðer on þæt heorðærn, his ham—

'Oh, don't you dare try and go down there - not until you tell me what you've done tonight. We have spoken about this. I need to know if you've left a mess anywhere.'

Silence. Down the streps to the basement.

'Listen, we can't have a repeat of Whitechapel. We just can't. And people are on edge now. There's a war on, I say!'

Se sceadugenga sits in the corner of the basement. The room is the only thing beneath ground floor in the house and is completely obscured. It's more of a laboratory than a room, but *se sceadugenga* only needs a damp corner. The apparatus is mostly medical, with some damp tomes on anatomy, physiology and surgery. Almost all of the books are out of date, but the Doctor had insisted on saving them when they moved to Battersea. The previous owners were an Anglo-French circus family called the Pinders. They lived in the house for decades until the Doctor and his companion came. The main owner was a man called Mr William Pinder.

The Doctor walks down the stairs. He looks around at his workshop with his dull eyes. He sighs and puts his hands on his hips, steadies himself from having to walk down the eight or nine steps. He won't live long in his condition.

'*Þær nis nán līc...*'

The Doctor straightens his cardigan. 'Well done. That's all I ask for.'

He walks back up the stairs, stopping halfway to catch his breath. His back is hunching over.

Mr William Pinder did not taste delicious. He didn't look it either. He had a drooping great moustache like an inverted "V".

His skull sits somewhere under a table with a damp tablecloth. A piece of paper falls on the floor from a nearby writing desk. It looks old and uninteresting, but more interesting than silence:

"Dear Mrs Freemantle,

3, Poyntz Road
Battersea
LONDON
SW11 5BH
16/12/1901

HOUSE HISTORY

I have just found the exact address of William Pinder; it was <u>22</u> Fairmount Road. By an odd coincidence I have just been doing jury service and one of the cases involved that very street: the area seems to have gone "down" since 1895!

There was also apparently a "Pinder's Mews" in South Lambeth. This might've been another of his properties, although I'm not certain. I enclose a modified page for your history incorporating the house number.

Yours sincerely, Robert Barkins"

'*Hwæt is þis?*'

The Doctor pokes his tired head through an illuminated doorframe at the top of the steps.

'What? What is that?'

'*Witung be Pinder.*'

'Oh, I had a former colleague from the Polytechnic Institute give me a dossier on our old friend, William Pinder. I needed to know if he'd be missed, et cetera, et cetera.'

'*Hwæt gif folc cume sēcan hine?*'

'Looking for him? No, that's the point in this letter. It's encoded. This isn't 1888 anymore and this isn't Whitechapel. The world is changing. We must be cautious, and if you cannot be cautious then we'll move again - probably to somewhere more remote like the Highlands or something.'

The letter is dropped in a small puddle in the corner of the basement.

The place where an arm used to be begins to ache, begins to pretend to still be there.

'What's happening?' The Doctor's voice is from the kitchen, where the smell of tea comes from.

'*Fals earm.*'

The Doctor always knows what to do when the place where an arm used to be starts to hurt. He knows how to make a balm to stop the itching and a tonic to calm the mind. It even works on *se sceadugenga*.

Half an hour later, the Doctor walks down the steps for the second time that night, huffing as he does so. He holds a silver tray with two vials. He begins to smooth one over the stump and the other is drunk.

It seeps down a gnarled throat, curdling like blood with syrup mixed in. The sound of dripping comes from a corner of the room. It hasn't rained recently so it must just be damp. Mould creeps in at the edges of the room, even making its way into torn tablecloths. The Doctor stifles a weak cough as he administers the last drops of the soothing balm.

'That'll sort you out, my friend. The numbness should last an hour or so.'

'*Ic þancie þē.*'

'You're welcome.'

The Doctor rises to his feet and shuffles around the room. The lantern is in his hand and rattles in his trembling grip. He has arthritis.

He has the means of procuring medicine for himself, but prefers to use his pension for his companion. It makes no sense. He will die soon and he hasn't gained enough knowledge for his sacrifice.

Understanding Old English is one thing, knowing of *se sceadugenga* is another, but he'll die as the only one to discover the truth, having gained nothing.

Perhaps he should be eaten when he dies.

Flæsc—

No, that would be disrespectful. His arms are weak and spindly. His gut sags and droops with loose flesh and organs ready to give out. His knees are mostly skin and bone and his neck hangs like a turkey's. Old men like him can look both fat and skinny at the same time, neither in a delicious way - none of the fat that renders, nor the lean to chew.

'You're thinking about eating me, aren't you old boy?'

'*Ānlic þonne þū dēad eart.*'

The Doctor laughs wheezingly.

'Well, it's awfully kind of you to wait until I expire naturally, but honestly I wouldn't mind at this point; everything aches fiercely.'

'*Hwæt meinst þū?*'

'What do I mean?' He always has a way of repeating the phrase back, probably to ensure he has translated correctly.

'What I mean, my friend, is that after four decades of research I have nothing to show. Yes, there are my findings as to your physiology and remarkable ability to not age - of which I must admit I am extremely jealous, especially these days - but what's a man of science to do when he encounters... something else.'

'*Þū sædest þæt sēo wīsdōm ealle þing mæge āsmēagan.*'

'That's true. I do indeed still believe science can explain everything, but science seems unready or unwilling to reveal what you truly are. All I have is fairytales, and the minute I take them seriously, I am doomed to the conjecture of mythology.'

'*Ic eom mōdcræft.*'

The Doctor laughs wheezingly again.

'That's true; you are indeed mythology, and that is the conclusion I fear will send me to my grave.'

He shuffles around some papers and scoops them under his arm. With his free hand he holds the lantern and escorts the phosphorescent light up the steps once more. He huffs as he reaches the top, and goes to drink his tea.

Se sceadugenga sits in the dark of the basement. The damp still drips. The mould still grows. The place is the closest thing to a marsh that can be found in London, the nearest imitation to a fen-lair. It seems like the Doctor has made it like that on purpose, to accommodate his companion, but maybe it's just good fortune. Not good enough, though. Nothing is truly like home.

Se sceadugenga slæpð—

* * *

Something lands at the foot of the steps in the morning. It's a strange time to be awake, so it must be the Doctor delivering something. It's a small and shiny box, with red in it.

"Redford's Navy Cut Cigarettes", "Manufactured by REDFORD & CO. London W.C.", "10 Cigarettes 10".

'*Ic þancie þē.*'

'You're welcome!' The Doctor is upstairs and rattling about.

'I'm going out again. Sleep well.'

Se sceadugenga slæpð—

* * *

Something disturbs sleep again. It's very annoying. It is like a distant bang, like a firework, only louder.

The basement appears unchanged. The dripping still sounds, and a heavy mist of sorts hangs about the ceiling. With the constant dripping, it's almost like mizzle—

Flæsc—

Flæsc—

No. It's daytime and there'll be nothing to eat until dark again. There's a smashed clock lying on the damp ground. The glass is broken, but the hands still softly tick. It's always few hours behind, but says it is still the early morning.

Maybe a rat might come down into the basement. They're easy prey.

There isn't much light coming from the top of the steps. The Doctor must have shut all the curtains incase *se sceadugenga* needs to walk around.

The first floor is a narrow corridor leading into a kitchen with little natural light. Even then, a stream of summery sunlight comes through a crack in a shutter at the end of the corridor. It burns.

The hall that leads to the kitchen is only slightly wider than the front door, and is cut in half by a staircase which makes it even narrower towards the other end of the house. The staircase has a white banister and leads up to the second floor where a bedroom is. The house has perhaps four bedrooms, but not much time has been spent above the ground floor. The wallpaper in the hall that leads to the kitchen is in need of redoing. It flakes off and has been like that for so long that cobwebs have formed in the loose flaps of mouldy wallpaper. The house is flaking into itself, and a perpetual mist of nearly sodden dust hangs in the dark air. A person wouldn't be able to see much in the dark light.

The sounds of something comes from outside. The murky window of the front door is blotted out with newspaper which has been stuck to it for the sake of darkness. But like the wallpaper, the newspaper flakes in parts and reveals veins of sunlight like burning blood vessels.

It hurts to look through them, but the sound of Macduff Road is growing more and more curious by the moment.

Squinting through the crack in the newspaper shows people gathered by the street, all looking in the same direction.

A police officer in his dark blue uniform and tall, conical hat cycles by.

'Take cover! Take cover!'

The police officer rings his bell and he calls out. The people on the side of the street look at him blankly. Around the police officer's neck is a sign.

"POLICE NOTICE" and "TAKE COVER" is what it says as it flaps over his abdomen.

The sound of his chiming bell and his voice carries off out of sight from the crack in the newspaper and fades off into the distance. The people around the street begin to move and heed the man's words. It's a strange sight.

Stepping away from the crack of light brings relief for the eyes. The sun can be so harsh. It can burn often. Perhaps returning to the basement, fen-lair, would be the best decision.

But the strange happenings outside and the distant, rumbling sounds make sleep impossible.

The house may be explored given that the shutters and curtains are all closed.

The kitchen's flooring is typical of a home in London at that time, according to the Doctor, with quarry tiles with checkerboard pattern, good for cleaning, were it not for the slime and rat droppings everywhere. The room smells of muck and damp. The Doctor lets the rats breed so his companion has something aside from people to satisfy himself. One of the tiles is upside down and has squashed insects protruding from it. The rats haven't got to them yet.

There is a single gaslight fixture for a light, held in by a thin cage-mesh and turned off.

The stove is for burning coal and is a black cast-iron covered in dust. It doesn't look very used. How the Doctor feeds himself is a mystery.

The stove is a "Kitchener" model and has an oven with long-disused hotplates. Utensils are hung up in the small alcove where the cooker sits, but have also gathered dust themselves.

There's a basin that was once white on the other side of the kitchen. It's porcelain with brass taps which, like the sink, no longer shine. It has a wooden draining board which has mould growing on it. It's not black mould but the kind which grows on food or *flæsc*. It smells of rot.

Flæsc—

Liðs—

There's a bucket of slop water beneath the basin which protrudes from a small, knee-high curtain concealing a cupboard with cleaning supplies which clearly haven't been put to use in years.

Above the basin there are cupboards for storage. They're all missing their covers and show their interiors. The skeleton of a rat lies face up in one of them, just next to tins of dried goods which people have been eating during this wartime. The Doctor hasn't touched them and *se seadugenga* certainly hasn't.

There's a wall-mounted dresser next to a pantry cupboard which is painted red. It's empty and its door hangs on its rusted hinged.

The previous contents of the pantry are spilling out like guts onto the slimy floor which makes squelching noises when its stepped on. Cracked jars with embossed tags which are damply flaking off leak flour. A perpetual mist of rot hangs in the air. To a human it would be disgusting, but the Doctor knows its a welcoming environment for *se sceadugenga*.

A wooden table in the centre of the kitchen has an oilcloth which is the slimiest thing in the room. Running a finger along its surface makes a fine line of green and black sludge. It's almost like mossy mud, like a bog. It's almost like home, like a fen-lair. It's never quite the same though.

There's a clock much like the one in the basement. It's made of enamel and doesn't work. It's stuck and broken on a time just before three.

There are checkered cotton cloths all strewn on the floor and wet as if they died in an attempt to mop up the filth. There's a sugar shaker and some empty spice jars mixed in with the dead cloths.

An hour has passed since the sound woke *se sceadugenga*. The sound of the sirens comes from the distance. They drone onwards and coalesce into a continuous whine. That, and the image of the strange officer earlier say that perhaps the zeppelins have returned, or something worse. Perhaps a bomb will land on the house. Maybe it will kill *se sceadugenga*. Probably not.

One item has been unobserved; it sits on the table and hasn't been touched in months.

Its a prosthetic arm. It is a combination of wood and leather. It's broken and the Doctor has left a screwdriver in it out of frustration. It was once used to replace the arm which is missing.

Maybe the Doctor will manage to fix it some day, but in his state it looks less and less likely every month. The man will probably die in a year or two... maybe less.

Maybe he's not coming back. Maybe that's what the sound was.

Maybe he's not coming back.

Perhaps it would be best to move then, without the Doctor? The prosthetic arm would have to be left behind, never fixed. Moving northwards would be the best idea. The Doctor said something about the Highlands. It's supposedly very far away. There will be places to go to in between perhaps.

But first, it is good to wait to see if the Doctor comes back.

CHAPTER 4
Whitechapel
1888

The streets are decaying.

Whitechapel is cold. Autumn is threatening to settle in throughout the city. It curdles the smog which thickens the air. In bogs and fens, autumn signifies the death of many things. It seems in London it is no different.

The streets are wide and black but shiny in the night. They are cobbled with grooves for carriages to go down. Not many carriages go down this area of Whitechapel. There is some degree of life though as it is Whitechapel High Street. Most of the windows are closed but a few public houses glow from their steamed windows. There was the constant sound of rowdy customers on street corners and a few on the high street.

The paving of Whitechapel High Street is uneven. Drunk people in their hats and coats stumble on the pavings, occasionally falling over and their friends help pick them.

Staying in the shadows keeps out of sight. The people are probably too drunk to notice anything anyway. People become very unwary at nighttime, even though it is the most dangerous time.

There's grime and litter on the streets and smoke rolls in from nearby factories. Many of them are closed for the night, but a few more essential ones keep making noise. They sound like distant droning.

The gas-powered streetlights are smothered by the fog or smog and have haloes around them.

The houses and buildings are pressed together. They look as though they are also decaying. There is "Alberts' Menswear Shop", but the sign is flaking off and there aren't any suits in the windows. "H. Levy & Sons" is next to the menswear shop. But only the pubs are making noise. People stream in and out of them in infrequent lines. Most who go in look like tired factory workers or dockworkers. They come out looking less tired and red in the face.

Standing in the shadow of a streetlight which has run out of gas because the lamplighter must've missed it, one can see the dozens of people who go to the pub. It looks like it's the only business doing well on White Chapel High Street.

"The Angel and Crown".

A sign hangs over the pub with the image of an angel and a crown. The Doctor had said that the reason they have pictures is because not everyone could read. But *se sceadugenga* already knew that.

The Angel and Crown is a large and dark building which looks like it has accommodation on the upper floors. The lights are all off except for the ground floor.

Se sceadugenga has never been into a pub before.

The sounds of all the people inside are the only indication of what it looks like, and the smudged outlines of all the people through the condensated windows.

The door to the pub swings open. Tobacco smoke bursts out like it's been trapped. A woman steps out and rests on the wall of the building. She looks drunk. She looks like she's catching her breath or cooling off.

She doesn't know she's being watched.

She is short and large. She has dark hair and it's tied up like women do in London. She has dark clothes on and many layers. It is a cold night. She tips her hat and looks up.

It's beginning to rain lightly.

It's beginning to mizzle.

Flæsc—

Ic wille tōslītan hire flæsc. Ic wille hīe etan—

No, not near the pub.

Laþlic—

Laþlic—

The woman goes inside away from the rain. The glow from the streetlights becomes dimmer. The cobbled streets look more slick and more uneven. People put their hats down over their faces and pull their collars up to their cheeks.

It's good as they won't be too observant with their heads down.

Flæsc—

"H. Levy & Sons - Fine Tailoring and Repairs". "Morris Haberdashery - Ribbons, Buttons, and Lace". "Branson & Co. - Ready-Made Suits and Overcoats". "Wright & Sons - Quality Meats and Provisions". "Chisholm's Grocery Emporium". "E. B. Harper - Fine Teas and Exotic Spices".

"Holmes & Rye - Freshly Baked Goods". "Stein & Co. Footwear - Shoes for All Occasions".

"Clark & Wright - Pawnbrokers and Loans".

Līðs—

Calm—

The mizzle weighs down Whitechapel High Street. The road

somehow grows quiet and louder at the same time. The place is muffled with water.

A few walkers remain out under the mizzle-haloes of the streetlights. Most take shelter in the pubs.

A stream of water builds up by the uneven pavement and slicks around the cobbles. The stream carries dirt and grime with it. A piece of rusted scrap metal breaks the flow of the stream in the gutter. Muck builds up in a small pool around it. The drainage system on the other side of the wide street is also blocked and puddles swell into pools. The mizzle doesn't form full raindrops. The surface of the pools shimmer with nearly imperceptible droplets falling. The sound is muffling.

There's nothing to be found on the street as long as the mizzle keeps falling.

Down Whitechapel High Street the other way, there are fewer things and people. In the daytime, the place is apparently more like a thoroughfare with shops and markets. In the nighttime everything is boarded up, everything but the pubs.

The "Ten Bells" pub is on another corner. It looks even busier than the Angel and Crown. The building is dark and hums with the sound people, of *flæsc—*

Liðs—

Two soldiers in uniform, both older and large men exit the Ten Bells. They seem jolly and sway on one another.

They both have large frames, but soldiers can be unpredictable. Their red uniforms look more like muddy brown in the mizzle-light of Whitechapel High Street.

They walk down the pavement nearly tripping every so often. They walk singing something unintelligible. They walk in the direction of the Angel and Crown. They walk as if drawn through the mizzle like moths to the glow of its windows.

A small bystreet with even more uneven cobbles than the high street is covered in shadows. Its dark and heavy. A person wouldn't be able to see in it.

Se sceadugenga can.

The door which feels more like a latch is opened.

Inside, through the small concealed door is a room which looks like it was once a stable but has been bricked up and abandoned for years. It looks like it has been a rat's nest for the better part of twenty years. Waste from rats and humans gather together on the floor. Wooden beams are rotting overhead. The sound of the mizzle cannot be heard from inside.

The sound of shuffling comes from an alcove. An oil lamp is lit and dimly glows. It comes around a concealing plank of wood and into the main part of the stables.

'Ah, you're already back.'

It's the Doctor who rubs his eyes at the sight of his companion.

'Sorry, I was just nodding off, actually. I say, what time is it?'

He looks at his pocket watch which is a dull, small thing made of what was once meant to pass for silver. He raises his dark, bushy eyebrows at the clock face. Recently he has been going to sleep earlier and earlier as if he were an older man.

Se sceadugenga knows that people often sleep later. The Doctor only looks about fifty. He has, however, been working tirelessly on his project.

'Look here, my friend.'

The Doctor walks to a table which has a crooked leg. The top of the table has screwdrivers and leather straps and springs and a selection of knives with different shaped blades. They are all blunted at the tip. The Doctor needs to buy a sharpener or a whetstone.

There is a prosthetic arm lying on the table. It is made up of cables in a poor attempt to mimic sinews, tendon and muscles. It is made of iron and steel with rubber and leather to hold it together. Cogs lock together around the shoulder and the elbow. At the end, where a hand would be, is a small blade which is relatively sharp. It protrudes from a wooden stump which looks like it's old oak burl, or maybe black poplar. Both trees are old friends. Maybe not friends. They are known though, and have been around for a very long time with *se sceadugenga*, that's for sure.

The Doctor holds up the prosthetic arm and manoeuvres it up and down, twisting at the elbow.

'Hwæt is þes to?'

The Doctor steps away from the table. He walks over to another, smaller one. He opens a book and looks at it briefly. A few minutes pass by with the Doctor mumbling to himself.

'Ah, I see what you're saying. Well, I'll tell you what it's for: you've been using your hand - which may I say, are truly effective and beautiful - but things are different nowadays. There are autopsies and investigators. By using this, whatever you leave behind will be mistaken for the act of a man, and not... well you know...'

'Þes is gōd ingehygd.'

The Doctor checks his book again on the other, smaller table.

'Yes, I believe it is a good idea. And this way, you may satisfy yourself on a larger scale without arousing suspicion of the supernatural.'

'Sōþlīċe.'

'Indeed.'

The Doctor takes the contraption and fits it around his companion. He moves carefully and flinches every time *se sceadugenga* breathes too near his face. His hands tremble every now and then. He doesn't blink as he fastens the buckles and straps around the shoulders. He steps back.

The prosthetic arm moves about freely. It is not like a real arm. It is like a weapon attached to the shoulder. It holds still and doesn't swing because of its elbow and shoulder hinges, but it's stiff enough that it can be thrust forward.

The Doctor reaches into his tattered pocket and takes out a rolled cigarette. He gives it to his companion, his subject, his friend and lights it for him.

'You know, I think your taking to smoking is what's kept me alive all these years.' The Doctor laughs. 'The minute you learn to roll a cigarette with one hand, is the minute you no longer have use for me.'

Se sceadugenga grymet—

'Oh, I'm sorry, I didn't mean it.'

The Doctor looks scared. He recoils away and towards his alcove with his oil lamp in his hand. He attempts to subtly reach around his waist for what is probably a weapon for self defence. It would do no good. But he is allowed to pretend he has a chance.

The Doctor holds his position, leaning against a cracked wooden beam that marks the entrance to his alcove. He tries to smile, but it is smothered by his fear.

'Perhaps… you ought to go test out your new arm…?'

It sounds more like a whimper than question. The Doctor is not a large man. For all his intellect he is easily spooked. Then again, he has good reason to be cautious.

The small hideout is left, if only to spare the Doctor any more worry.

The mizzle has subsided outside. The wetness has settled into a nighttime shine on the muck of Whitechapel High Street. People walk along the streets in their coats and mantles as if it is still raining. The smog hangs thick over the streetlights and weighs the air down. The buildings drip slickness onto the badly guttered street. The breadth of the high street is filled with a thin filament of water, like a puddle as wide as a river thats been broken up by uneven cobbles and human waste.

The river is still and unmoving. Perhaps, if all the people left and never came back, the streets of Whitechapel would become like a marsh, like a bog, like a fen-lair eventually. Would the muck and slime build up over the stones? Or would the stones break and reveal soil and dirt underneath which swallow the cobble.

The street holds firm and the buildings don't fall. Both look like they might soon enough. Buildings were stronger and less rotted hundreds of years ago in place like Cologne. In Whitechapel, hundreds of years later, no improvement has been made except the number of people.

The stairs make small splashing sounds with footsteps.

There are many backstreets and alleyways off of Whitechapel High Street.

Leman Street cuts across in a straight line. The roads intersect to make a junction. One can see all the way down Leman Street. It is less busy than Whitechapel High Street but also narrower. There are fewer people walking down the wet streets as well.

The Angel and Crown looks just as busy as before. The windows are fogged up and the sound of people comes from within. The doors come open again.

Tobacco smoke bursts out like its been trapped. The same woman comes out amongst the smoke and sound, straightening her dress. She realigns her hat and begins to walk easterly down the street.

She looks plump—

Flæsc—

Flæsc—

There are other people around. One man walks on the other end of the street. He looks like a tired labourer. He tips his hat to the short and stout woman as they pass.

Remaining in the shadows on the other side of the road keeps things alright. She thinks she's alone.

Two women pass her. They are talking about someone named 'Margaret' and laugh loudly. Their laughs fill the street and they walk into the Angel and Crown.

The short and stout woman with dark hair keeps walking. She moves drunk, but keeps her rhythm on the uneven pavement. It looks as though she's done this walk before, or maybe adept at walking drunk in general. She takes out a hip flask and swings from it. Her hips move side to side. She huffs every few steps.

The weight of the prosthetic arm with the knife on its end sways gently. It's comforting. It's balancing.

The woman is met by another, who stands outside the White Hart pub.

'Alright, Pearly Poll?'

The other woman who was waiting has two men with her. They all four greet each other. The two men look like soldiers. They are not very tall or dangerous-looking. One of them has a rifle with a bayonet. Pearly Poll appears to have been the woman who was waiting. She talks with the man with the rifle and the bayonet and they walk away. Pearly Poll leads him down an alleyway.

The short and stout woman is laughing gutturally with the other solder. He too has a rifle which he picks up from leaning on the side of the pub.

The short and stout woman with black hair takes the soldier by his free hand. She walks him through a very narrow passage beside the White Hart.

It is the passage which leads to George Yard and onto Wentworth Street. It is an old yard which is closed at night and easy to go through whilst unnoticed.

Se sceadugenga had used that yard to sleep in once or twice - before the Doctor and the stables.

The doors to the White Hart come open. Tobacco smoke and steam pour out along with the light from within. A man is thrown out and into puddle with a splash by two larger men. He slumps in the dirt and lies still for a second.

He looks like easy carrion for a moment. Then he splutters and gets to his feet. It takes about two minutes of stumbling until he stands, which he does with his feet very widely set. He walks in the direction of the Angel and Crown, dripping dirty water and swearing.

Whitechapel High Street grows quiet for a moment. No people walk down the street except for a few very far in the distance. It's peaceful. The silence is perfect.

The smog hangs low.

Flæsc—

The narrow entrance to the alleyway has sounds coming from it. Heavy breathing.

Flæsc—

Heavy breathing. Brick archway. Cobbled pathway just wide enough for a wagon. Shadows. Shadows and breathing.

Flæsc—

Shapes moving in the dark. Pushing. Sliding.

'What the bloody hell was that?'

The soldier's voice is laboured. He's a heavy set man. Raspy tone. The shapes stop moving for a moment. Heads move around in darkness they cannot see through. They don't know they're being loomed over.

The breathing begins again.

Líðs—

It's a curious scene. Staves off hunger. The shapes slide in the wet of the mizzle which came before. They sound strange. It's unusual. It's unsightly.

George Yard is made of bricks and cobbles. It is more narrow and less practical than one would imagine. It's a long stretch of useless road onto Wentworth Street. Only the soldier and the woman are in the yard. The hatches and windows of the buildings are shut. No sound comes from anywhere, not even Whitechapel High Street.

'Cheers, love.'

The soldier stands and fastens his breeches. He takes a coin from his jacket pocket and gives it to the woman. He picks up his rifle and bayonet.

'You leave first, guv'nor. You're just a soldier patrolling this here street. I'll come about in a few minute.'

'Cheers, Martha. See you later.'

The soldier slings his rifle over his arm and walks out into Whitechapel High Street.

The woman wipes herself down. She puts the coin in a pouch and adjusts her hat.

Shadows deepen in George Yard. The smog seems to drop just a bit. The night thickens and weighs heavy. It's as if the mizzle falls again.

'Eh? Who's there?'

'*Hāl þū.*'

Ic bīte into flǣsc. Hēo is swā wāc. Ic stice hīe. Ic stice hīe. Ic stice hīe. Ic stice hīe. Āgēan ond āgēan. Āgēan. Ic ontyne hīe ond tēo hyre flǣsc tō mīnum mūðe. Hēo is mīn mete ond ic eom hyre hunta.

Hēo spæcð tō cīegean. Ic lecge mīnne mūþ ofer hyre ond bīte niþer. Hit is heard þæt ne bīte hyre hēafod of. Ic sceal brūcan þone earm. Ic slīce hīe. Ic stice hīe eft. Ic stice eft. Stice eft. Stice.

Þær is blōd ofer mé eall. Fæger. Hāt, wynsum, weleg blōd. Ēalā, hit is swā wundorlic. Hū lufie ic þæt bæðian on manna blōde. Hit is swēte þing. For mīnne earm ic wille ofslean þūsend þūsendra manna ond wīfmannena. Ēalā, hū atēlic ond blīwlig ond winful ond fætt is þæs cildes lāþe blōd, ac hit is mīn tō genimenne eall swā same.

Líðs—

* * *

George Yard is slick with blood.
    The city is quiet again.

The short and stout woman lies open on the floor. The knife at the end of the prosthetic arm is broken. The entire arm is broken. The springs hang loose and dislodged.

The alcove is heavy with shadows and blood. The chiming of the early hours from a distant church bell rings through the smog.

The alley has tenement flats on the western side. A few have their lights still on. The sound of a fiddle being played comes from an open window. The mizzle starts again. It settles around the black alley and to the northern end where Wentworth Street is. The top of a large building which is Toynbee Hall is shrouded in the mizzled smog.

There's no one near the alleyway. Not a soul disturbs the quiet place. The mizzle drops and hangs in the air. The blood curdles in the open wounds.

Out into the mizzle, *se sceadugenga*.

CHAPTER 5
Bastille
1789

The air is weighty near the Seine.
Paris is weighed down heavily by the scent of blood. Most of it is charred or rotting, malnourished.

A dark alcove in the manmade banks of the Seine. It looks like the entrance to a sewage tunnel, but it's made of crumbling brick and mortar. A dented cannonball lies in the mudbank by the river. It's low tide. The water has retreated but it has left the smell. The drip from inside the tunnel echoes out shyly through the night. The ripples of the river move sluggishly down through the city. Pieces of driftwood and other human waste scatter along the banks.

A body slides along the river. It's facedown with its limbs spread even. It looks bloated around the torso but skinny at the limbs. It's wearing rags and has slime over its skin. It comes close to the hole next to the Seine.

Wading through to retrieve it, the water feels cold. It's always cold in the Seine, especially at night. The moonlight reflects off of the brown river and the slimy skin of the body drifting in.

It's dragged to the bank. It's stiff.

Turning it over, the face looks like a peasant, but the cheeks and mouth are bloated and purple. The eyes are closed or swollen shut. It's hard to tell.

Flæsc—

It's not ideal, but it's abundant in Paris.

Ic ete þæt rottene flæsc. Hit smæcð yfel. Ic hæbbe to fela deaðlicra līchaman geetan. Þæt flæsc is swilce yfel wæter. Hit is yfel þære tunge. Hit is yfel þam steortan. Ic ete and asende þone līc aweg. Hī wencað þæt rætan þæt flæsc geeton.

The remains of the body are sent floating down the river. It will land somewhere near the Notre Dame.

It won't be the only body in the Seine that night. They've been growing more and more in numbers recently. Some of them are malnourished. Others are soldiers. Very few are in good condition.

The sky looks smooth like a starless pit. The moon is alone and almost full, but not quite. The city has sounds of singing and fighting at the same time. Sometimes it's hard to tell the difference between the two.

The low tide Seine makes a sloshing sound. It slides like blood thats being drained through the city. It sounds thick and coagulated.

A soft breeze makes a low whistling sound through the mouth of the hole in the bank. It looks like the mouth of a large creature with no teeth. Perhaps the teeth have been shattered into the rubble and the cannonball which is beginning to rust.

Inside the hole, the walls are brick. Moss and slime grip the bricks. They make the once nobbled bricks and stones smooth and wet. Dripping from the concave ceiling sounds and echoes every few seconds. Squelching of feet sounds with each step. Again, echoes of the sound travel down the tunnel. The sewers beneath the city aren't in use anymore. They're just places for rats to live in now, and other things.

The tunnel winds and has many offshoots. There were once vagrants who slept in it to avoid the crowds which gather on Paris' streets. Only one inhabitant stays in this sewer now.

A few rats scurry from some decaying twine. The smell of their excrement fills this section of the tunnel.

The tunnel travels for miles with nothing in it except the occasional body or large family of rats. Very close to the entrance is a large grate which can't be moved by people. It lets moonlight in and occasionally the sound of people talking can be heard from it. Tonight it is silent.

An old and crooked ladder leads to it. It is just strong enough to support the weight of *se sceadugenga*. It's awkward and noisy to climb with a missing limb.

Wiping the mouth of rotting *flæsc*, one can peer through the slits in the gate. There doesn't look to be much.

The gate is opened slowly at first, then shunted aside. It makes a scraping sound but doesn't seem to disturb anyone.

A courtyard stretches out in the moonlight. It is very wide and long and looks exposed to the elements. Around the grate there are cobbles but the courtyard looks muddy and cold. The entire building around the courtyard has eight towers which look like they are made out of stone. They're very tall and broad. Between each tower to another one are tall walls.

The silhouette of a man moves slowly along the top of a wall with a musket slung over his shoulder. It looks like he is wearing a hat which belongs to a soldier. He is patrolling like a soldier does.

In the courtyard there are barrels, crates and scattered pieces of equipment. Some of them are tools like hammers and nails and wooden planks. There's a chisel for stonework half-buried in mud. Perhaps it is for repairs to the castle, *se berg*—

On each of the towers are small, barred windows. There are two barred windows on each of the eight towers. Four of them have candles lit which glow softly from the inside. The faint sound of a man singing comes from one of them.

Not much time has been spent in this place. It's cold and basically uninhabited.

Smoke comes out from one of the roofs of one of the towers. It blackens the sky behind it like a pillar coming from the shallow, pointed roof of the structure. Beneath the chimney with the smoke coming from it is a large, unbarred window. Shadows from moving figures move within it. The shadows look as though they are pacing.

There are only two soldiers patrolling the walls and no one is inside the courtyard. Aside from the soldiers, the singing and the shadows, there is nothing to indicate that the building is in use. It looks more like a ruin.

It's a place to explore... to hunt.

One of the towers is the Rue Saint-Antoine which is in the Faubourg Saint-Antoine district. It is busy in the daytime with marketplaces and lots of people.

The tower which is close to the Rue St-Antoine has a voice coming out from it. It starts and stops in irregular patterns like a drunk person singing.

The tower is made of smooth and large stone bricks which look several hundred years old. It rises very high and is broad, like it could be a singular building on its own.

Is þis palentse—

No, it can't be a palace. The soldiers walk like guards and it is too abandoned to have *cyningas*—

To have kings in it.

A figure steps from a large archway which is decorated with simple stonework. It looks like a man, and he is wearing a fine uniform. A human wouldn't be able to see in nighttime, even with the moon, but it is clear that the man is not tall, nor is he young. He walks with a cane in his hand. He looks nearly fifty. He's wearing a wig.

A younger person walks beside him. The assistant, for it looks like a young assistant boy, carries a candlelit lantern. It needs refilling. The boy holds it at the feet of the older man so he doesn't slip in the mud. The older man keeps a hand on his assistant's shoulder anyway.

'Mais, gouverneur, pourquoi sommes-nous ici si tard?' The assistant's voice is squeaky like a rat's.

Enough time has been spent in this particular land that

the language is understandable. They speak like water flowing, but sometimes the water snags on rocks and sounds harsh. The people can be the same way, but they taste like all others.

The assistant seems to want to know why they are walking around so late.

It is curious.

'Parce que Pierre, la prison est faible et a de nombreuses failles. Je crains que le peuple ne tente d'y entrer. Un informateur m'a rapporté que des fauteurs de trouble projettent de prendre cet endroit d'assaut. Ce n'est probablement qu'une rumeur, mais il serait prudent d'inspecter.'

The man speaks in a way as if he enjoys the sound of his own voice. He sounds older than he looks. They walk around the walls and stand at specific parts. They don't speak when they do it.

'Faites-moi votre rapport demain matin. Je suis fatigué et trop vieux pour cela.'

The old man lazily walks away. He yawns and disappears in the archway where he came from. The young boy, according to the old man's words, must stay and report to his master in the morning. It seems strange, it's not his task is it?

Regardless, the young boy walks around the courtyard. He almost slips on some mud. He holds his lantern up to certain parts and writes down on something.

Se sceadugenga leaves his hidden place of watching.

The boy can neither see nor hear the unwelcome guest. He never would. No human can do so at night.

The boy looks young and strong and healthy.

Flæsc—

Flæsc—

The *forroten flæsc* of the other bodies is different. It's not the same. Enough has been consumed for the night, at least until the next one.

But *flæsc—flæsc* like this...

Flæsc—

'Qui est là?'

The boy whirls his dying lantern.

He is too slow to catch what was behind him.

Þa sceadugas—

The shadows, they are a cloak

Sceadugenga—

The boy stands motionless and peers out into a darkness. He cannot see.

He still looks scared, though. He looks so scared as if he saw what stalks him. But he couldn't.

He is probably the sort of child who believes in ghosts and other monsters.

He'll learn that certain things are real.

Flæsc—

Closer...

Closer...

Living, agile prey is always different. It can cry out. It can run. They never get far but it's always messy.

Flæsc—

It will be over quickly.

Ic grip þone lytlan cniht. Ic stinga mine clawu into his muð, and he ne mæg sceamian. His eagan wiðuþ, þæt ic him eallunga forþan to slægenne, and drincþ his blode. Eala, hu swete and frisce is his flæsc! Eala, hu wundorful! Hu mære! Swa swiðe deor is feor þæt ic hit gemet in þa stræte of Paris.

Ic hæbbe þa lænan dæl to læte.

✻ ✻ ✻

The moonlight looks peaceful.

The lower half of the boy is dragged to the grate which is left open. He's very light. It's like dragging a rabbit. The legs splay like broken branches and make a crunching splat as they reach the bottom of the hole. It's hard to tell if it's the mud or the blood which makes the sound.

The sun is still an hour or so from rising.

It's strange. It is very beautiful and bright, like blood which catches moonlight.

But it always *bærnþ—*

It always burns.

It's a strange sensation. Being tortured by something beautiful is what a mad *skald* once described as love. He was an odd thing indeed. Humans always are, just as cattle are to them. But that man was truly weird.

Wyrd—

The sound of a dog howling comes from the distance. It sounds like it's being tortured. The howl turns into squeal. Perhaps the people are eating it. It would be wrong to judge them. But somehow judgement towards people comes all the same.

The dog stops howling. One of the guard-soldiers walks along the top of one of the walls. His silhouette moves slowly and he has no idea of what's happened under his watch. He probably won't ever; mud and blood mix well together.

For a city which is noisy and full of bloodshed and rot, it's very quiet at night.

The sound of the singing voice comes from one of the towers again. It's a very curious sound. It's like wailing. It's like crying.

The tower encroaches into the courtyard. It can be climbed.

Climbing stone walls is difficult. It's not like climbing cliffs or mountains. It's more like trying to swim through mud; it's not meant to be done, but it's possible.

There are cracks in the stone bricks and gaps in the mortar which allow for a claw to fit in. It is better to climb the dark side of the tower than to do otherwise and alert the guards. The stone is crumbly. It's not quiet. Air grows colder higher up. There's a small breeze.

Closer to the window, more noise is made from the singing voice.

The window is lined with iron and iron bars cut across its face. They would perhaps not be too difficult to rip off, but it would make too much noise.

Peering through the bars, there's a candle in the centre of a room. The room is in a circle and people sit in it. There are seven of them and they don't move much. They are like statues in the still air. One of them has shackles around his ankles.

One of them is trying to read a book, which is tattered, by using the one candle in the room. He uses a monocle which is cracked. His hair is white and a wiry grey beard brushes the floor.

Another is a young man who is fat. He snores loudly but the other people don't seem to mind. There's a man drinking from an old, foggy bottle. He sings. It sounds more like moaning. The other people don't seem to mind.

They'd all be fine prey.

Flæsc—

But it would make too much noise to get them.

Looking outward from the side of the tower, high in the air, the city seems quiet. The air is clear except for a few chimneys in the distance.

A massive cathedral rises in the distance. It's taller than all the other buildings. It's been called the Notre Dame sometimes.

It's a foul ode to *God*—

To their saviour, *Hælend*—

To their lord, *Drihten—*
To their creator, *Metod—*
To their ruler, *Wealdend—*

So many names for one thing. *Se sceadugenga* goes by many names as well, all of which chosen by people, by those who fear; except for *sceadugenga*, that name is good. It is true.

The Notre Dame is dark and piercing. Perhaps to people it looks beautiful. There are other tall buildings but none as big as that one.

One of the guards stands on a scaffold on another tower. He has his hands on the wooden bannister. He leans over and looks towards the tower across the yard.

Mæg hē mē geseon—

No. Even with very good eyes, a person could not see *se sceadugenga* in the shadow of a tower at nighttime.

But he peers with such intensity and curiosity like a dog that has seen a hare.

Looking up at the wall which is being clung to, the moon has dropped down. Twilight is coming. The sky bleaches itself before the sun comes. The air is brighter.

Perhaps the guard can see well enough then.

The tower is descended, the courtyard is crossed and the hatch is closed up behind all within a matter of seconds and in complete silence.

Shadows linger enough in twilight that still conceal.

Down in the sewer tunnel, the remains of the boy are submerged in mud and slime. Rats scurry away from eating at the ankles when *se sceadugenga* enters.

The rats are cowards, but at least they are smarter than people, than humans.

Þa legu sind fordigde. Bita be bita hi beoð fornumene oð þæt hi fyndað fostor. Nis micel belifen, ac hit is genoh for þa niht, and se sunne cymð sona—

Líðs—

It's time to settle in, for the sun rises and tries to creep in through the tunnel. Its burning, blinding warmth searches out all dark things and dark corners and dark hearts. It is conquering, colonising, consuming.

Deeper into tunnel where a stream of rats flow, picking teeth with a young boy's bones.

* * *

Once more, sound disturbs sleep though the daytime is not done, and the need to hunt has not yet come. People will never tire of making noise.

A blanket of mud and slime has wrapped itself over *se sceadugenga*. It's like a fen-lair, like the far away home.

The slime is pushed aside and limbs are stretched out wide, cracking. Rats stir and scurry. Some of them seemed accustomed to their guest, knowing he is sated enough to not have at them. Perhaps one should be devoured, just to remind them. This is why rats are smarter than people.

A blasting sound echoes from the city through the tunnel.

Small currents of dirty water cut through slime and mud. A rat skull dams one small stream which is rust-coloured.

The smell of smoke comes through a soft breeze from the tunnel's entrance. It doesn't smell of smoke from wood or bodies. It smells of smoke from gunpowder, the black soil which turns to flame.

A clapping sound comes through the tunnel. Deep in the tunnel's bowels, it's hard to tell what distant sounds are. It swallows, muffles, echoes noises until they become like every other sound in the tunnel. Distant droning sounds come through the tunnel. It's enough to rouse curiosity.

The sun is shining harshly through the open hole in the side of the Seine. Light shouldn't be able to reach and root out the shadowy parts of the place, but it curls around the bending passageways of the sewers.

The slick, sludgy, slimy rot-walls of the sewer tunnel become silvery like gems closer to the entrance. It's too bright to exit, but something's happening outside.

The sounds which grow louder and louder don't seem to be coming from the other side of the Seine.

Perhaps the grate will show more.

Deeper into the tunnel is cooler, more at ease, more like *niht*—

More like night.

The water rises a little the deeper in. Less light means it's easier to see. Less sun is calmer, better.

The place where an arm used to be begins to ache. It throbs.

Hit byrð—

It burns.

Laþlic—

Flæsc taken by prey. So stupid. No sense in it. Waste.

The grate near the ladder deeper into the tunnel lets light through it. It hits the mud beneath which swallows it. The light looks like a pillar. It looks like a pillar of fire which holds still.

Sound comes from it. It's too bright to come near.

'Mais, monsieur, je l'ai vu! J'ai vu un vampire! Pierre a disparu aussi!'

The voice isn't one that's been heard before. It sounds like a young man. He seems concerned about seeing a monster in the night.

'Silence! Il y a une armée là-dehors, bon sang!'

The tone of the governor comes from up top. It is the same raspy one from the previous night. He seems worried about an army being near.

That must be what the sound is. It sounds like a droning of hundreds of peasants.

They sound angry.

That will be much *flæsc*—

But too much perhaps.

A nearly picked-dry bone of the young boy is by the base of the ladder. It pokes out of the mud. A rat gnaws on it like there is no noise nor people around. Cannons softly sound in the distance.

It is safe in the tunnel.

It is safe in the dark, for now.

CHAPTER 6
Calais
1558

The town's outskirts smell putrid.

The sea, which is called the Channel, throws up salt on the walls of Calais. The air is heavy and the ground is wet from rain.

One side of the city is a harbour on the outer side of the wall. The walls are tall and stone, always manned by soldiers. The walls have battlements and structures. Sounds of voices always come from them, often officers speaking orders.

The wall meets the ground at the narrow stretch of harbour. Tents and huts and shacks make up the structures. A few houses are in ruins. This particular part of the port is not used anymore.

Soldiers from the inland attacked and destroyed it. The tents are sagging and wet. The shacks are inhabited by rats and crabs. The huts which were once baileys are now just rubbled wood.

It's the perfect place for *se sceadugenga*.

Some bodies were still left untouched by rats. There's not much left now.

Moving along the shoreline, the sound of waves under wooden promontories and platforms bounces off the tall city walls. It's hard to say whether or not the port is part of the city, or a growth. Ships from the northern side of the Channel often enter. One sunk when it was hit by a lightning bolt a few miles out to sea. The soldiers gathered along the wall to watch. *Se sceadugenga* sat at the bottom. It was not that interesting. But it was interesting enough to remember. Or maybe nothing happens in the eastern side of the port, which is now a ruin.

A cloth lies in the mud between two burnt pillars. Six golden lions and six golden flowers look dirty and damp on it.

A malnourished dog walks over the skeleton of a soldier. The *flæsc* on the body has rotted but a rusted helmet hangs over the eye sockets of the skull.

The dog would be too fast to catch.

Flæsc—

There's no point. It's early evening and the town behind the tall wall is quiet.

The dog seems to sense the thought. It runs away out to the

beach. Its head goes up and down and it's scabby fur glistens in the wind It runs along the beach eastwards until it becomes a speck kicking up wet sand behind it. It leaves prints in the sand.

The moon rises over the shoreline where the stray dogs runs towards. Some dogs can run faster than wolves. One of people's strange concoctions, that and the giant stone wall.

Sometimes the only option is to go inside, over the wall. It's easier now that the people from inland are attacking; everyone has gathered behind the walls for safety, thinking it will help.

Walking among the ruined structures is easy. Often there are stray people who are peasants who walk by. But they never make it out.

Walking along the walls, many stones are cracked or lichened. The place looks strong and ready to crumble at the same time.

A pile of barrels and crates stack on top of one another. They've been jammed open for looting. The contents have spilled out and look like twine. The looters must've left disappointed.

The shape of a hooded man walks just ahead.

Stepping into the shadows, it's easier to watch and see what he's doing. The figure walks half-drunk, half-mad. He holds a crucifix up in the air. A horrible thing.

He walks amongst the destruction but keeps looking up towards the walls. He looks up three times in two steps. He comes very near to his watcher, of course without knowing it.

He stands with his dirty, dark robes. He is a bearded man but has cut the hair on the top of his head. He's a monk or a priest or a missionary or whatever it is that people like to call themselves under their... *god*.

The man bends his spine to look up the high walls of the town.

He cups his hands to his mouth and takes a deep breath.

'Écoutez, écoutez, l'sieur, not' père, connaît les péchés d'ces Anglois. Chés soudarts n'sont point d'même force qu'les anges d'Dieu. Repentez-vous et levez-vous, compaignons d'pays!'

Not enough time has been spent in this land to understand what he's saying, but it seems he's imploring people to rebel.

'Hold thy peace down yonder!'

The voice which responds comes from the top of the wall. Perhaps it is a soldier. The priest, who looks old and who's bald head catches the moonlight, looks as if he doesn't understand what is said to him. He keeps walking as if drunk.

He could make for prey.

But the crucifix...

They've hurt in the past. Churches and cathedrals, both evil.

Almost as evil as that night in Cologne—
The moon climbs higher in the sky.
The madman with the crucifix keeps walking through the mud, moaning as he does so. His robes are baggy and his voice is slurred. He looks half-dead. Maybe he is drunk on death. He smells of blood and gangrene. He leans over to throw up. Something slick and almost solid comes out and splats into the mud. It's hard to say what's wrong with him.

He wanders away to where the port is not destroyed. He'll probably be shot by an arrow before he reaches the water.

A sword in the dirt catches the moonlight; it's already rusting.

A ship has been anchored a stone's throw away from the ruins. It looks abandoned. There are probably merchants on it waiting to see if the siege holds before trying to sell their goods.

A crow lands on the protruding pommel of another sword, its pointed beak flicking back and forth. It's a dark creature, and an old friend.

Crows are friends of wolves, and wolves are known to *se sceadugenga*. It looks at the lone one, the *anhaga*, the *eardstappa*. Its head cocks sideways and it blinks its eyes which glint slightly. Its feathers are ruffled in the wind and it caws again.

'Hāl, frēond.'

It looks confused, doesn't respond.

It's been too long since the fens, since the *mere*. Even crows aren't friends anymore.

It flies away, flicking its head in search for carrion.

Moving through the wreckage, the high walls of Calais curl around wide towers which have the sounds of soldiers coming from their battlements.

Thousands of tents gather on the southern side of the town. A few fires flicker among them.

There looks like there might be twenty thousand people gathering in front of the town walls. Bits of cloth showing who's fighting whom flutter in the nightly breeze. The town wall facing the army has the lions and the flowers from the wall.

Above some of the larger tents are the symbols.

There's a long blue one with golden flowers, three of them.

Another is very complicated. It has two lions, flowers, stripes and crosses overlapping each other. A person wouldn't be able to see what all the shapes are from afar, even in the daytime.

Another is red with two golden lions. It looks like the one from the English.

There are many others in different sections. It's a quiet night with a small breeze. The sounds of soldiers talking carry on the wind in the direction of the town. It probably scares the soldiers who are watching the attackers.

There are large wooden towers constructed in triangles with extending arms. They look like sleeping giants in and amongst the army. They have been the ones hurling stones at the wall.

The wall has holes and cracks and wounds in it. It still stands but it has only been a few days.

Se sceadugenga has never seen stones of such size thrown at stone walls. It's not clear whether or not it should take years or months or weeks, but the whole town smells of fear.

Perhaps *flæsc* can be found in among the camp of the army.

Perhaps that is too risky.

There's a long and shallow crack running up where a round tower meets the wall. It's must be one of the weak points in the defence. It's good for climbing.

A claw fits in the fault easily. Small stones drop down softly on grass below. Not much sound is made with the ascent. It's difficult to do with only one arm, but the feet can be used for their claws, even teeth where necessary.

The air grows cooler and the wind a little stronger towards the stop of the wall. It is the eastern side of the town, so the moon shines on it, but there's no one near enough to see.

Only crows can. There are many in the distance. They know what is to come, what has begun.

The top of the tower has no roof and no guards nor soldiers. The stone battlements rise and fall in continuous patterns, unbreaking.

It looks like a circular platform or a stage which sometimes people use to perform to others. The stage of the tower on the walls of Calais has a very large audience of people, perhaps twenty thousand or more. They're silent. They don't applaud or laugh or cry. They wait for the climax of the act. That is probably the only thing which interests them. The large wooden towers look tired from the fight. They will likely be used the next day and the day after, until the walls crumble and the stage is rushed.

From on top of the tower the inside of the inner town becomes visible in the light of the night. There are lots of platforms and walkways behind the lower walls which have soldiers on them. They gather in small groups of three or more and speak. Their voices sound like distant mumbles in the still air.

The people in the town have their own bit of cloth with their own patterns and colours. They all look the same really. One which shows on houses and hanging from windows in towers and off stone walls is a white sheet with two red stripes crossing each other. Some are like the muddy one from before, the lions and the golden flowers. They look very like the ones from the army outside the walls of the town.

The tower is a good vantage point. This is how crows must feel from on top of trees or buildings. Many small shapes of small people move like shadows through the dirty streets in between houses which are black and white with paint and dark wood. There are probably more people outside the walls, waiting to come in, than there are in the entire town, inside the walls and around.

There looks like many soldiers with their symbols of the cloths that they wear and with weapons in the belts resting on their shoulders. They all look tired.

There are a few horrible churches in the town. Their spires stab at the sky. They are grey and soulless. There is light from all of their windows and their doors which are open. People gather in and around the churches from the look of it. People do such things when they're scared. It's weird, a *wyrd*—

So much *flæsc* gathered in one place. But it is all untouchable.

Something must be had before the night it over. There's only so many places to take shelter in the daytime and the walls make it difficult to get to people.

Even people can spot silhouettes or blank spots in the night sky, so descending is best. The inner side of the walls and the towers has many staircases and ladders. It's easier to get down. There are people though, mostly soldiers. There are not that many. They make noise in their metal, their armour-clothes and they can be avoided.

At the bottom, the houses look bigger and the streets look wider. There are a few small passageways between the houses which smell like they are used as latrines. The town smells of disease and fear.

They fear the wrong things.

Flæsc—

Flæsc—

It's difficult to move through the town without people noticing something is wrong. They move to churches or somewhere else with things in their arms. They seem restless but quiet at the same time. A priest walks down a wide street and chimes a bell.

'Domine Deus, refugium nostrum et fortitudo, qui populum tuum in tribulationibus...'

There has not been enough time to learn Latin. It is a language for very few people which are hard to get to, and the church which is harder to get to.

People look up as the priest walks by, ringing his bell and speaking Latin. Most look to him hopefully. The rest of the people look at him blankly.

One building which is black and white like with others with paint and mortar and wood stands alone in a small square. There is no one in the area.

A dog barks in the distance. It sounds frantic. Perhaps it smells something it doesn't like. It's far away though.

The house has a window which has its shutters open which has a dull light coming from it. It's on the ground level.

Approaching, there is the sound of soft breathing. It sounds like a man's.

Through the window and into the building is a small room with a candle which is about to burn out. There is a soldier slumped in the corner and drooling on himself. He limply holds an opaque bottle in his hands. It looks like he forgot to extinguish the candle before sleeping. Maybe he didn't mean to sleep at all.

There is a bed with blankets which are brown. There are two chests which are light brown, and hanging from the wall, above the sleeping soldier's head is a wicker basket and a leather satchel. There is a jar of straw on one of the chests and the soldier is barefoot; his shoes are on the bed and have flaked dried mud onto the sheets.

His soft heartbeat shows in his bent neck, a throbbing vein beating alongside his gentle breath.

He looks like a soldier because of his clothes with the symbol-pattern on it and the dagger in his belt. There is a tall spear leaning in the corner of the room.

There are tools of iron next to the window. They are rusting.

The ceiling of the room is thick wooden beams and the walls are pale and grey. It looks like a room which would muffle sound.

Flæsc—

It was careless to leave his window open.

Flæsc—

The window is narrow. It's difficult to squeeze through. It could fit a small person in it but even a large one would struggle. The windowsill squeaks but eventually the window allows the intruder in.

The bed squeaks like the windowsill did but louder.

The soldiers eyes open.

The candle is almost out.

His eyes widen.

Flæsc—

The soldier grabs his opaque bottle tighter and throws it. It misses its target and flies out the window. He scrambles to the spear, stumbling as he does so. He looks amusing. Perhaps he deserves a chance to fight back.

'Get thee back, ye fiend!'

He's almost brave.

He stabs his spear into the shadow at his window.

Se sceadugenga smiles as the spear shatters.

The soldier draws the dagger and screams. He doesn't have many teeth and the ones which remain are black and grey. He runs forward.

Perhaps he is brave.

His dagoras brecað.

Ic gripige his earm and rippe hit of mid minum tēoth.

Ic et hit onforan him, þonne he wāt, to wērdan his mōd. Hē spītt blod. Ic spitte his agen blod on him. Ic et hine fram fōt to healf. Hē hlypð eallunga þæt ic rīce his byrst. Hē smēlt gōd. Hē smēlt of wīn hē drincþ und blod þæt ic drinc. Hit is god mete. Soldēra ēac smēlt gōd. Ic rippe his cīep of to forlēosan mine mete. Ic et þæt læstan of him. Hit is god mete.

Liðs—

* * *

The sound of other soldiers make it necessary to flee.

The guard is only a blood stain. A trail is left through the mud of the town and even up the walls of the tower.

Se sceadugenga has the soldier's head and is on top of the tower from which was entered. It was difficult to carry the head in the mouth but the one available arm is needed to climb.

Atop the tower, the town of Calais and the city of tents and campfires look peaceful again. The people move about quietly, little shadows in the muddy streets and around the tents.

The head of the soldier looks like it's still shocked. Holding it in the palm of a hand, in which it fits, two pairs of eyes look to one another, perhaps both are as dead as the other.

The soldier's mouth is open, revealing his limited number of teeth. He has a faint moustache of black, wiry hair and whiskers on his chin. His skin is pale and his hair is knotted and thin on top. It's hard to say what people like, but this man does not look like people would call him handsome. Maybe soldiers are ugly.

His eyes are grey and wide open. He is silently screaming. Blood still drips from the place where his neck used to be and a gullet dangles on the floor of the tower. The stage is now bloody.

The head is always a strange part to eat. *Se sceadugenga* never knows which bit to start at. It's almost like an apple - turn it around until one part which is much like all the others looks worthy of biting. The first bite is always the most difficult.

The head is eaten.

The crows circle around the tower like vultures. They see well in the dark like *se sceadugenga*. They don't know, however, that there is no *flæsc* for them to eat, unless they suck at the drippings on the tower and down in the mud. People's eyes would not be able to tell the difference between mud and blood. They cannot smell it either

The wind slowly picks up. It is cold. It makes the cloths which bear the symbols of tribes and kingdoms flutter loudly. Apart from that and the distant trees, there is no movement in the town's houses and walls and sheds and ditches and squares, nor in the encampment's tents and spikes and horses and fires.

The night has become cold and the moon is covered with clouds which glow silver at the edges when they come together.

It is time to go. The soldiers which walk along the battlements and platforms seem to think something is wrong. They turn away from looking at the army and into the town.

A bell chimes.

It is not the bell of a church which is a horrible sound. It sounds like an alarm. It comes from the building where the dead soldier used to dwell.

No doubt they will tell stories of ghosts or rapture stalking the streets and sucking their blood.

They're not wrong.

But neither are they right.

CHAPTER 7
Cologne
1349

There are fewer and fewer people in the city each day.
    Sometimes *se sceadugenga* wonders what he is, tries to imitate a people's sense of what they call morality. In the city, much has been learned about people. Much of it is ugly.

The city reeks of buboes, pus and sepsis.

A small unnamed street has been a place to live in peace for a time now, but the streets are growing more and more restless.

The buildings in the small unnamed street are made of dark wood and whitewashed walls. The roofs are steep with clay tiles and sometimes thatch. Uneven cobblestones make up the ground.

There are barrels and crates on the floor. Many of them are cracked open and have been looted. The fingers of a severed hand protrude out of an opaque puddle. The palm is hidden. The sound of sheep being led through the city comes through the small unnamed street.

People don't deviate from the main roads very often.

The sound of people singing follows the shepherd and his sheep.

'Maria, hilf, du reine Maget, Du Trost in aller Not, Zu dir wir Sünder flehen, Bitt' deinen lieben Sohn…'

The voices trail off and are swallowed by the quiet of the night.

The people in this place have a strange language.

It sounds very similar to the language of the singer-bard, Gleoman—

He is gone now.

The language of the people here sounds similar to him, but different. People will be hard to understand. But it will happen in due time.

Moving through the small unnamed street to its entrance, it's easier to see the people.

They still move around at night which is surprising. People didn't always do that. There was a time when the sun fell they generally kept to their settlements and houses and halls and huts.

But this place is different; it is what the people here call a "stadt", which probably means city.

Maybe twenty or thirty people walk up and down the street at a time. It is a very dense street with tall buildings but narrow roads.

A woman walks down the road with herbs in her hand. She holds a scarf over her face and wafts the herbs, which look like rosemary and thyme. It looks like she's trying to swat away an insect. There are others also with things covering their faces. People keep very distant from each other. One man coughs and spits out phlegm and bile into a puddle.

People stare at him and he hurriedly walks away.

A dark and shadowy figure moves through the thick air down the dark street. It is tall and black. It has an assistant which looks like a young boy who is sick. He coughs heavily.

The tall and dark and shadowy figure is wearing black clothes and wears a mask. It looks like a crow's head with red eyes but much larger. People move to the side of the road and let the figure and his assistant pass by.

The assistant is pulling a small cart. There are bodies on it. The limbs smell of *rotung*—

They smell of rot.

Flæsc in the heaps. Every day people like the shadowy figure and the assistant pass by with *flæsc*—

None of it can be eaten.

It is foul. It is *laplic*—

They are *wætan*—

They are pus.

They are *blōd*—

They are blood but not the kind for drinking, congealed.

They are *ādle*— *untrumnes*— *lēgesēocnes*—

They are disease, weakness and pestilence.

They are *plege*— *mānseocnes*— *wælcyme*—

They are plague, sickness, the-slaughter-which-comes…

So much blood and *flæsc* and people wasted. They are taken out and disposed of beyond the city.

Hunger for *se sceadugenga* comes and goes when it wants, but the bodies are carted away. Even the people who are not sick are at least malnourished. They don't have enough food.

The only good thing is that people keep away from others. It's easier to single people out when they are willingly alone. The only way to get it is patience. Patience is sickening.

A group of people walk down the street together, which is odd.

They are only wearing bits of cloth around their waist and groin. They hold frayed rope in their hands and chant things as they walk.

The other people with things wrapped around their mouths don't move to look at them like they did with the tall shadowy figure and his assistant with a cart full of bodies.

The place where an arm used to be begins to hurt.

It is ignored, the people walking down the street are interesting.

They all look very skinny and do not have enough *flæsc* on them. They are barefoot and have blisters on their dirty feet. They, all in unison, take their frayed ropes and thrash themselves on the back. They do it again. They do it again. They do it again.

They don't stop as they move down the street and people don't stop to look at them. The sound of their whipping is rhythmic and one man leads the chant in their strange language. There are maybe fifteen of them. They keep their eyes forward to the end of the street and don't show the pain. The small of their blood is curdling, rousing.

Their backs drip with fresh, peeled *flæsc*.

The drip falls into shallow puddles in the cobbles and darken the water.

They move down the street and the sound of their chanting and whipping fades away as if they were never there.

People are strange.

The night is still young and like the street, which is poorly lit with torches and moonlight, the stars look bright and cruelly beautiful.

※ ※ ※

The street eventually clears up of shadowy figures and naked people with whips.

Patience is sickening, but too many people in one place can be worse.

A church bell chimes its horrible sound in the distance. It sounds like its mourning people. That is a strange idea. How could a stone building or the metal bell inside it mourn people, living things?

An old woman carries a basket walks down the street hunched over. She is wearing brown and grey clothes and has shoes with holes in them.

Her smell carries through the still air and her soft, pattering heartbeat sounds weak. She is not prey for the night. As easy as it would be, there is no point in following her.

The tall and shadowy man with the mask like the crow walks down the street in the other direction from when he came before. It may or may not be the same one, but there is no assistant and no cart.

His red eyes on his mask are unblinking and his heavy breath sounds muffled in his leather beak. He holds something in his arms and walks carefully like he's trying not to disturb it.

It is a small cage with frogs in it. They look blankly at the world around them and blink. They hop over one another every now and then, mostly when the masked and shadowy figure takes an uneven step.

He will make good prey.

The sound of a real crows comes from somewhere overhead. There's no sight of them against the starry sky; they are even better at hiding in shadows than *se sceadugenga* sometimes.

The shadowy figure is walking carefully and slowly, his attention on the cage of frogs in his hands. He's perfect to follow. Perhaps under his dark clothes there is *flæsc* in abundance. There's only one way to find out.

The street only has dangling oil lamps and the occasional torch in a metal holder. Apart from that and the soft light from some windows, the shadows have taken over the buildings.

There is no way a person could tell they were being followed.

The wet floor from previous rain makes the cobbled floor more like a fen, a marsh, a *mere*, and that is a place where stalking is done best.

The shadowy figure walks in the shadows, unaware that one of them is following him.

The person walks through an abandoned square which is busy in daytime. People put up their wooden tables and give others their products in exchange for silver and gold. People are strange.

Stranger still is the shadowy figure which walks with his frog-cage as if it's a normal occurrence.

The square is surrounded by tall buildings. One of them is a church. It has several pointed spires. It stabs at the night sky.

The church is silent. Maybe it was the one making noise earlier.

On the other end of the square is another one of the shadowy figures. He's holding a torch which is blazing brightly. He has inspected a body which is lying down on the side of the street. It almost looks like a kindness, were it not for the shadows and the mask and the torch.

The shadowy figure in front keeps walking, trusting that he doesn't lose his footing in the dark. To his credit, he hardly missteps and moves almost as if he is nocturnal.

Timber houses with exposed beams and whitewashed walls rise higher to where the shadowy figure stops.

All the candles are out and there is no light aside from the stars and the moon.

He puts the cage on the floor. The frogs start to make noise and hope around more. It's like they can sense the wetness of the floor and their closeness to it.

The area where the houses are taller and the street is broader looks abandoned, except for the shadowy figure and the one who stalks him.

It looks as though the shadowy figure with the mask has gone into this alleyway so as not to be seen. His breathing grows heavier.

The shadowy figure grabs his mask by the crow-like beak and pulls it off his head like it's a hood. His breathing sounds louder. He seems unwell.

He bends over and splutters bile and half-digested food into the mud. He coughs several times and spits out blood by the end of it.

It smells putrid.

His breathing grows heavy in between coughs. He clutches his chest and groans.

Hē is sēoc—

The shadowy figure, now without his mask, whirls around. His face is covered in buboes and his skin is covered in black sores. His left eye is almost completely shut with swelling and there's blood on his chin. He looks helplessly out at the shadows around him, the moon failing to light the place well enough.

'Wer gât dâ?'

It's not clear what he has said, but *se seadguenga* reckons it to be a question as to who is out there.

Flæsc—

No. He is rotten. He is dying a poisoned...

Flæsc—

The smell of his blood and bile fills the nostrils.

Mid ānum earmum ic his swūran genime.

'Got errete mich,' he says.

Ic þrēate, and his hēafod sprincð of. Hē bersteð swā fūl frēolīc wæstm, and sē dēaðes ādl mid him ūtgœð. Ic ne mæg geswīcan. Ic þearf etan. Ānlic hit mē þurhteōn þæt ic swelte.

Ic slīte mid mīnum tōþum þǣre stōwe þǣr his hēafod ǣr wæs, and ic drince. Ic hæbbe nān oþer weġ, nān ġeweald.

Hit is yfel mēte.

Līðs—

* * *

The night has grown old and the little street which has no name has been retreated to once more.

Se sceadugenga holds his stomach with his one arm.

The stomach churns, rejects what's been eaten. It bubbles and broils and burns in the depths of the bowels and abdomen.

Laþlic—

Laþlic—

There is fire in the belly and nausea in the head. The street which has no name swirls and spins around and the houses and buildings rock. Bubbles of hot, carnivorous gas pop from the mouth and smell like rotting flesh.

'*Egesa! Egesa! Mōdor, hwǣr eart þū?*'

It is stupid to call out. People might hear. What's more, it's more stupid still to scream out for *se sceadugenga's* mother. She is dead. She has been for a few hundred years now. There's nothing she can do. There's nothing *se sceadugenga* can do.

But surely a human illness cannot kill that which is not human? Surely?

There's no other choice but to wait and find out. There are no sores and no pains and no coughing - only belching and bubbling and bawling.

It has been a few nights and yet it feels like a thousand days, days in the hot and overbearing sun.

The feeling must be waited out.

Perhaps starvation will come.

That would be a foul way to die indeed.

The place where an arm used to be aches as well, pretends it's still there.

The illness must pass.

It has to, *Gleoman* had said as much.

He was a wise, wise, strange man.

'*Ic wille on life wunian.*'

CHAPTER 8
The Mere
500s A.D.

The night is cold and the winter remains.
The shoulder where the arm was ripped off is throbbing. It pulses like hot blood is trying to reach something which isn't there. A bandage wrapped around the wound reddens with old and dried blood which is dark like rust. It smells like rust too. It is the only thing which smells in the fen-land, the *fenhleoðu—*

In the summer and the spring and the autumn and all the seasons unknown to people in between the others, there is smell and stink and odour and putrefaction in the swamp and fens. In the winter, it freezes and the smell of slick wood and slime and dying things stops, grows hard.

The only thing in the cave in the *mere* of the fens that has odour is the shoulder of *se sceadugenga*. It smells of gangrene. It smells rotten and infected.

Maggots coil and churn in the *flæsc*. They gleefully tear into the *flæsc* of the flesh-tearer.

The drip from almost-dead moss comes from the roof of the cave and spiderwebs are frosty and dew-gripped.

The sound of winter birds comes from outside. Crows caw and cough as if they have caught the scent of carrion. A trail of blood must have been left on the ice around the *mere* and through the stagnant mud and sludge of the fens.

It sounds as though the animals are rejoicing, congregating for the mortal wound of the dark one, *se sceadugenga.*

The barking bugles of fen-harts and nattering foxes echoes through the morning.

The sunlight streams through the cave entrance and bludgeons the aching head of the dweller in the hole in the earth, in the mud, in the swamp and fen.

The sound of something approaching comes from outside.

Perhaps it is the one who took the arm, come to finish the job? That would be a kindness, a mercy indeed.

Laþlic—

Loathly…

The footsteps from outside the mouth, the dripping maw of the cave, sound like it is something with two feet, not a deer, or a wolf from the fens hoping to get an easy meal.

A head pokes out from the entrance, blotting out the horrible winter sun which blinds.

'*Þes hāl!*' The voice of the newcomer is cheery.

It is a man who is young with brown hair. His eyes are wild like a madman's but he speaks softly. He carries a lyre in his hands and has a thick, wintry cloak around his shoulders.

'*Ic gretie þé,*' *se sceadugenga* says. The voice is weak, dying even. Regardless, it's good to see a familiar face.

The man who enters with the lyre calls himself Gleoman. He, with a strange smile, sits down on a mossy root protruding from the side of the damp cave. He looks at the creature before him.

'*Hū ys þīn earm?*' asks the young man, gesturing to the wound in the shoulder.

Se sceadugenga does not respond. It is clear Gleoman knows it is not good - he is the one who bandaged it.

Gleoman plucks at the strings of his lyre. He frowns at the sound which comes out, echoing in the dripping cave. He plucks each string methodically and twists something at the neck of the wooden instrument until the sound winds up and contorts itself to his liking. He then plucks again and smiles at the sound it produces.

'*Gōd,*' says Gleoman, setting down the lyre by his bare feet. His toes have turned black and his ankles are swollen. He is strange-looking, even for a person.

He looks at the cave-dweller with a kind of pity and mourning. His eyes well with tears but he blinks them back.

Se sceadugenga does not understand what the emotions are, but Gleoman has spoken of *lufu*, which he explained means love.

The poet-shaper has taut *se sceadugenga* all he knows about how to speak his tongue, *Ænglisc*, with which he writes his poetry and songs. It's a crass and harsh tongue, but it is the first and only language which *se sceadugenga* has known. He can now articulate himself, if not to loathsome people at least to himself.

It helps at times.

Before, it was just actions, just doing things like the way the wind blows and does not know why; the way the sun horribly shines and doesn't care what it gazes at; the way the sea churns itself and throws storms at the land as if it has a mind, but it does not.

Se sceadugenga has a mind, he just didn't know it until he knew language.

It is a strange sensation - to know words.

It is the one thing which people do well, aside from taking up space. They make patterns and things which did not before exist.

They take the land and till and plough it until it makes patterns and the patterns give them food. They take wild animals and make them domesticated and patterned. They take forests in the wonderful randomness and make patterned structures like *Heorot*. They take the natural sounds and make them into patterns and shapes and sequences. It seemed stupid and pointless until Gleoman taught the words.

Now they can be used to understand the self, to contain the self and reason with the self.

Se sceadugenga wasn't even sure he existed until he knew how to say it.

'*Ic eom...*'

I am...

Maybe too much credit is being given to Gleoman - he is just a person after all. People just die in the end or are eaten. That's all they're good for when they serve their purpose.

It's never been clear what drives the young person.

He says often how he is not from this land, the land of the Scyldings. He says he is from a distant place across the sea...

'*Englaland...*'

Even so, it sounds guttural and strange.

Gleoman looks at *se sceadugenga* with a gentle gaze.

'*Englaland?*' he says, raising a dark and bushy eyebrow.

Se sceadugenga nods.

'*Far þider...*' the young person says, smiling.

He makes a good point. Perhaps *se sceadugenga* should go to this *Englaland...*

It would be away from the likes of the people who tear off arms. They might even assume that the monster from the fens is gone. That would be a kindness.

But it would be hard to move through the realms of people without knowing them. They are so strange and odd. Perhaps, now that one of the languages is learnt, more can be learnt by listening. It would take many years, many aeons. It might be worth it. There has to be a place for *se sceadugenga* to take refuge. The fen-lair is no longer safe. The *mere* will be hunted. *Se sceadugenga* will be hunted.

'*Caines cyn*,' says Gleoman, as if reading the mind of the silent beast before him.

Se sceadugenga almost laughs at the statement. The kin of Cain - that is what it means. There is no way of telling if the statement is true or false. People are strange with their poetry and their metaphors and their images of fancy. As Gleoman had once stated, Cain was a person, much like himself, full of this thing called "sin" - a ridiculous notion of not acting like a god.

But *se sceadugenga* has always felt that he is more like a god than any of the weak and weary people from the likes of Heorot who claim to be like their precious Father.

'*Caines cyn...*' he utters to himself, affirming the poet-shaper's accusation.

The two laugh together, their strange, unmixing voices echoing through the cave.

Silence comes over them and they sit in it for a time.

The shoulder begins to throb again. The wound is only a few days old. In the coming nights it will become clear whether or not it will be a mortal one.

Death would be a strange way to end life. That is a fate reserved for people, not *se sceadugenga*.

Gleoman seems to grow tired of the silence and takes his lyre in his hands. He looks at it lovingly, the way he looks at *se sceadugenga*.

He thinks a while and is watched by his host for the duration.

He opens his mouth and takes in a deep breath, his eyes on a distant, non-existent thing as he does so.

He then breathes out in the form of what he calls song, poetry, shaping patterns of language...

'*Oft him anhaga
are gebideð,
metudes miltse,
þeah þe he modcearig
geond lagulade
longe sceolde
hreran mid hondum
hrimcealde sæ
wadan wræclastas.
Wyrd bið ful aræd!
Swa cwæð eardstapa,
earfeþa gemyndig,
wraþra wælsleahta,
winemæga hryre...*'

He trails off his voice which is like a songbird and lets the last syllable be swallowed by the dark maw of the cave. The words settle on the undisturbed slime and mud and cobwebs.

The words might've one day been as foreign and untranslatable as the singing of a bird, heralding the morning sun.

But now, now he knows their meaning:
"Oft, the solitary one
finds grace for the self
in the mercy of the measurer—
although he, sorrow-breasted,
must for lengthy times
row down waterways
of the icy coldness of the sea
and tread exile-paths.
Fate does as it wills!"
That seems laughable, but nevertheless...
"So spoke the earth-treader,
aware of woes
of wrathful slaughter
and the ruin of kin-friends..."

Gleoman looks at *se sceadugenga* expectantly, as if awaiting his translation to be complete.

He receives only a slight grunt of approval.

The young poet-shaper gives a dejected look.

Silence takes them over again, settling like a winter.

Se sceadugenga is tired. Sleep descends like a swooping hawk. He is weary from fight and wounds. The fear that this will be the last sleep ever had settles in. But sleep comes like fate, like *wyrd*. It cannot be stopped.

The last thing *se sceadugenga* sees is Gleoman picking at his lyre as the cave grows dark. Then refuge from the sun is taken.

❋ ❋ ❋

It is not the last sleep for *se sceadugenga*. It is easier to see when it is nighttime.

Moonlight comes through the mouth of the cave and the insects and bats and birds of the night have stirred from their daily sleep.

A night like this would be good for hunting for *flæsc*.

The shoulder-wound aches and throbs, burning fire and ruin. The maggots squirm in their feast. It's hard to say if the blood and ruined sinews are poisoned or healing - both hurt.

An owl hoots somewhere out in the swamp and a wolf howls further in the fens.

Exiting the cave, the scene looks peaceful. The marsh and bog and swamp and fen which surrounds the cave gather together in a mess of dead and rotting land. Beyond, the *mere* shimmers in the moonlight. The water catches the silver— *seolfor* like a net full of white fireflies.

A bog-snake slithers away at the sight of the one-armed monster above it. Its dark head plunges into the ever-blackness of sludge.

Ice glistens at the edge of the mere and where the mud comes to points, like frosted spear-tips pushing a taught, brown sheet up to the sky.

Something disturbs the death of the *mere* in the distance.

No person could see that far, only wolves and hawks and *se sceadugenga*... and his mother.

But she is on the other side of the *mere*.

Is that her, protruding about the edge of the water?

No.

It is a person, a man. He's moving, searching, hunting.

Does he come to finish the job he would otherwise presume is done? Or does he search out the birther of *se sceadugenga?*

Perhaps it is Gleoman, but he doesn't usually come out at night; though he doesn't fear *se sceadugenga* as other people do, or did. He still stays away from the wolves and the bog which is more dangerous.

A movement startles. It bursts through the fen-foliage like a leaping fox.

It is Gleoman. He waves his arms above his head, flapping like a madman.

'Ryn!' he cries. 'Ryn!'

And so, *se sceadugenga* obeys.

He runs.

He runs far and hard away, to who knows where...

CHAPTER 9
Heorot
500s A.D.

'**M**īn earm! Mīn earm! Mīn earm!'
Blood pours in great spouts from the shoulder, a breach in the giant flesh-frame. The shoulder muscles have sprung apart, ripped by some Geat, some mere person. It is horrendous. It is horror.

The bone-locks hang loose in the place where the arm used to be. Blood spurts out from snapped tendons and pain-like-fire licks and crackles in the place where the memory of an arm is.

'Mīn earm!'

It's no use. There is no one to hear, in the white snow and the black forests, for anyone to hear the cries. There is no one.

Anhaga—
Eardstappa—

Blood spurts into the snow. The frost and hoar and ice drinks the blood with pain of its own. Steam rises with hissing sounds as the tendrils of thick, curdling, roaring blood sink deeply and carve red ripples and ridges into the resting snow.

The virgin snow...

It almost looks peaceful.

But blood, blood!

'Mīn earm!'

The pain is unbearable. It is a mortal wound, it must be. How could it have happened?

Never— never in all of middle-earth has such a hand-grip been felt, by man or other.

That should never have happened. It's wrong. It's a mistake...

The shoulder which used to hold an arm burns and aches and throbs.

Blood pours out like vomit, squeezed in sizzling pain and hurled against the owner's will. Instead of a mouth it comes from a ruined socket, a mass of entangled tendons and *flæsc* and pain.

So much pain...

The cool wind blows over the wound and the trees and the snow and the mountains in the distance.

Darkness hangs everywhere and a company of devils laughs

everywhere like crows cawing in the blackness of night.

The fen-bordered layer is beyond, beyond with many steps from the horrendous Heorot— the wine-hall of Hrothgar and his host.

Behind, the glow of the open door of the hall glows gently, and laughter sounds from inside. The hall stands at the top of a slope and has houses and pens around it. It is tall and dark like morphed wood come together to make a cocoon. The cocoon laughs with the sound of people. They laugh and cheer their saviour and take pleasure in the knowledge that their hunter, *se sceadugenga*, flees to death.

Even the wind jeers. It knows that its bastard offspring will likely die in the coming days. Heorot is bugling horns and the wind and the crows; they all make a celebratory choir, a chorus of people and things all averse to *se sceadugenga*.

The banqueting-hall of Heorot is made smaller and smaller as the snow is fled through, out to the wilds.

Great tufts of snow are splashed by rough knees and the cold bite of the icy hoar has no effect. The night is cold but the wound of the shoulder is hot and heavy.

'*Mīn earm!*'

The voice comes out through the wilderness. Mother won't be able to hear.

'*Mīn frēond!*' a voice calls from far away.

It is Gleoman. He is somewhere in the woods like a fool.

A person should not be out in the woods in the night. Then again, *se sceadugenga* should not have been in Heorot, where the Geats were waiting for him. A trap.

The light of a torch on fire comes from between the shapes of the two large pine trees. They look like sentries guarding a lost and wandering lamb.

Gleoman is wrapped in his clothes which look like they are not working to hold away the cold of the wind. His torch is flickering and smoking as though it is about to die.

'*Mīn frēond!*' says the young man.

Se sceadugenga winces at the glow of the torch, but there is no way a person can see at night without it.

The young and mad poet-shaper's eyes widen with shock and horror at the sight of the wound at the shoulder. Blood spurts out as if on cue, and splats with a sizzle on snow resting on the branch of a pine tree.

'*Mīn earm...*'

Gleoman looks at his torch and looks at the shoulder. He looks back and forth a few times, as if thinking something.

'*Hwæt?*'

Gleoman does not answer the beast which asks.

The torch is pointed like a spear and thrust at the place where blood spurts out.

Flame and blood do not mix well.

'*MĪN EARM!*'

Gleoman does not stop. He pushes the flame harder and harder into the wound. *Se sceadugenga* resists swiping away the small man, ripping his head off, tearing his throat out.

'*MĪN EARM! MĪN EARM!*'

It's all that can be said.

Gleoman persists.

❋ ❋ ❋

Mizzle settles from the sky like heavy snow. It thickens the air and dampens it. Mizzle-haloes and the murk of water-that-is-not-rain come down like tears.

They do not weep for *se sceadugenga*, who weeps in place of the sky, *heofon*.

Sleep does not come easy once the two friends reach the cave through the *mere* and through the fens and the marshes and bogs.

Once the wound was burned to hardness, the flame went out and Gleoman collapsed to the floor. He would be eaten by the fen-wolves if left there.

He doesn't deserve to live any more than any other person, but he at least did a favour and deserved to be carried away from the wood where he would surely die, having just prolonged the loathly life, or the death, of *se sceadugenga*.

Gleoman sleeps at the back of the cave where his scent will not be caught through the slime and the dirt by any wolves or worse, the mother of *se sceadugenga*.

She may have heard the cries of her son; she may be soon to wander out to Heorot in vengeance; it will be an ill-made journey, like that of the first.

Se sceadugenga, his shoulder bandaged with fire, sits almost peacefully at the maw of the cave with the fen in all directions.

The mizzle descends.

It comes down and down and down.

It never stops. It wets the wetland and dampens the damp.

It is like mockery.

It is like death.
It is not clear what will happen next.
All that can happen, all that is allowed, is to wait in the mizzle.
The horrendous, ever-falling mizzle.
It shall be a reminder of the night.
Mizzle.

CHAPTER 10
The Highlands
2025

The land is dry.
The A82 is a road which cuts over an industrial bridge with iron girders which are grey and somehow always dry, even in the rain. The bridge is called Ballachulish and cuts over Loch Leven. It separates North Ballachulish and Glenachulish.

The place which the locals call Glencoe is very beautiful, by human standards. It is a narrow valley, a glen which cuts through the land with forests and high points of stone which are nearly mountains but more like hills.

A few islands are more like promontories at the edge of the loch, which itself goes out to sea, stretching and broadening to openness. The sound of birds can sometimes be heard, and near the roads there are cars or even people walking around, happily wandering a wilderness they have made safe for hundreds of years.

Se sceadugenga stands near the B863 which cuts along the northern side of the loch. It is at the feet of mountains which go white with frost in the winter, but not too cold.

A few houses gather to the side of the B863 with small gardens. They are whitewashed with grey slate roofs and dark windows. Thick bushes blockade the three or four houses from the steep slope of the mountains.

A wooden gate is left open because not many people travel this area compared to Edinburgh and Glasgow to the south. A strange tree with dark, upturned leaves stands next to the open gate like it's keeping watch. The tree is young though, and hardly looks like its more than a few decades old, if that.

"Burnside" says a sign next to the open wire fence of barbed wire, just above a few rocks placed strategically to hold up the gravel gateway and support the gutter running along the road at the same time.

The land here looks very rustic and yet catering to other people walking around, driving around.

Perhaps it's not the ideal place which the Doctor had said it was. Maybe it's too far south in the hills and mountains and lochs but at least it's better than the south.

It's only been night for a few minutes, and the windows of the houses by the B863 are still on.

People and their *flæsc*—

No.

People would surely notice someone missing here. Temptation must be avoided.

The road is abandoned and could be walked down. If a car drives now it normally drives fast - but they'll just assume that there's a deer darting off the road. They always assume something they can comprehend; "common sense" is what they call it, so said the Doctor. Gleoman called it *ġepōht*—

Reason.

There's a mossy cobblestone wall running along the northern side of the road and black and white bollards running along the left. They look reflective, and catch the glint of *se sceadugenga's* eyes from the moon, which pokes out from heavy clouds overhead.

Further down the B863 is a lay-by which looks like it needs its potholes fixed. Opposite is a wooden fence which looks quite new, hardly worn by the elements.

The trees all look old and yet the woods don't quite look ancient in this part. Thistles grow where there's space for sunlight or moonlight to come through. Leaves rustle in the breeze.

Dying bracken to the right and the gently flowing loch to the left. It is a calm place. A beech tree slopes in an inland direction.

The distant sound of something comes from the west, up the B863. A halo of light comes from over the treetops which shroud the winding road. Rubber on tarmac roars in the distance and grows louder.

Moving to and amongst the dying bracken is the only option. It crunches under a claw.

Lying down in the undergrowth, two headlights can be seen careening down the bend in the road. The car sounds like a constant whining from steel and rubber and tarmac. It shrieks onwards. Its eyes never blink nor deviate from the direction in which the large, metallic beast travels; metallic it hurries on; metallic it leaves its red lights in its wake. It moves like a startled cow, unable to comprehend its action nor its size nor its purpose.

The bright headlights trail on through the woods like a lonely, wandering lighthouse in search of the sea.

The B863 goes on and on, further than it has any right to through the woods and the ditches and the dykes and the fences and the bracken. Tarmac carves alongside the loch.

The town of North Ballachulish is coming too close. There is a slope to the north where people can be avoided. It is covered in stumps of recently felled trees. Branches of birch trees are strewn up the side of the hill which comes to a point. The ground is soft and hard to climb without slipping.

At the top of the hill, Loch Leven can be seen. It stretches along for miles. It grows broader and broader towards the sea as if it's a massive river, but the people call it a loch, in their harsh tongue which sounds a little different to the ones down south.

Looking the other way, where there are fewer houses and people scattered like stray sheep from a flock, there is a pathway which looks like its made of dirt and dusty gravel. It cuts through a valley which is halfway up one slope of another, much larger valley.

The hills and mountains look like they've been folded up and over one another until the rules of understanding what are dells, glens, valleys, dales and hollows are no longer rules. The green and the black and the grey of the Highlands are like giant waves frozen and lichened before the moment they each impact one another to send their spray out into the sky.

The pathway which cuts through the small but high up valley is pleasant to walk on. It makes a gentle crunching sound which breaks the silence of the vast land. It's easy to see, even for a person probably as its paleness winds through the dark hills.

The ruins of what looks like an old smokehouse or shepherd's hut stand alone on the side of the pathway in the moonlit shadow of a large slope with craggy rocks protruding from it.

People talk about that spot. Its walls are standing but it has no roof and serves as more of a milestone than a true structure.

It looks lonely and sad, disused and dilapidated. The people call it Tigh-na-sleubhaich.

It means something in their native tongue, but for some reason they don't know what it truly means. It's clear what it is though. It's a very old house which is made of large stones which are gripped by moss and lichen.

People might walk past it in day, but by night it is as peaceful as anything.

Hungor—

Hunger comes forward. Perhaps the Doctor was wrong. There is nothing here for *se sceadugenga*.

Blōdlust—
Ānnes—
Wlæclic—

Bloodlust, loneliness and loathsomeness - that is what is to be found in this place.

Was it a trick? Something the Doctor said to try and save his companion from devouring too many people? There's nothing here.

A deer moves over the top of the hill. Deer are stupid, but they can sense things better than people can. They can run faster too. They make for difficult prey. Open hills and rocky slopes are poor hunting ground for one accustomed to prey on people.

What was the Doctor thinking?

This place is north of Gleoman's home... *Englaland*.

Perhaps they were both lying. People shouldn't be trusted, even though they seemed like friends at the time. Of course, they're both gone now. All people go, whether by eating or in their own, fleeting ways.

They're so weak and that's probably why they trick. But do they trick?

The Doctor was odd, true, but he was no liar. A liar doesn't devote their life to a deception. Gleoman is a bit more strange. The Doctor made sense; people and their sciences do all sorts of things. But Gleoman was what his contemporaries call an artist, a poet-shaper. They do not do things of such madness, unless it is for what they call love or passion.

Frēondscipe—

That is a concept which *se sceadgenga* was not made for.

Mother was not one to be loved, not in the way in which people do. The fens and the marsh and the bogs and the land is not one to be loved. Not even the cave can be loved. Friendship is a thing selfishly guarded by people. Even when they try to bestow it upon a beast they do so only to enrich themselves, and like madmen they seek to love that which cannot love them back.

It is like how sailors love the sea and farmers love their fields. It is like how scientists love their experiments and drivers love their cars. People are strange and willingly make themselves into weak things.

Even here, at the height of hills and valleys, the people have scattered themselves, scarcely coming together to make a community, and yet they insist. They love their land, but their land does not love them back.

Almost one and half thousand years has been spent attempting to understand and coexist with people. There have been those who beg; those who weep; those who fight back like the three in the alcove at Newcastle; those who run; those who try to call for help. They all do the same things at the end but when they are not in danger they do all sorts of different things.

Which is a better representation of people: the version when they live peacefully? Or the version when they die?

Both are just as real as the other.

People are strange.

They don't know bloodlust nor do they know true hunger and loneliness.

What does it say that the only two who would know *se sceadugenga* are madmen. Only madmen are capable of anything, and even then they fade away like all the rest of them.

But... the whole, the group, the hoard, the cities and towns... they live on. It's like they are a hive of ants. To kill one is inconsequential, even to them. The hivemind of people lives on forever and always. They will never die.

And as long as they live, *se sceadugenga* will live also alongside.

'*Eom ic brōþor?*'

Whether he is a brother to people or not, he is there. Maybe more of *ān sceadu*—

The one that is *sē genga*—

Se sceadugenga, out in the open air.

Somewhere in the distance, mizzle descends.

GLOSSARY

The main source for the language in this text is Michael Alexander's translation of *Beowulf* as well as Seamus Heaney's, *Sweet's Anglo-Saxon Reader* (15th Edition) and Elaine Treharne's *Old And Middle English: An Anthology* with some help from www.oldenglishtranslator.co.uk. Some of the translations in this glossary are based in poetic interpretation rather than linguistic ones.

Technically, there was no centralised lexicon known as Old English. Much of what we know is thanks to Alfred the Great (849 – 899A.D.) who likely set West Saxon as the mainstream. There was also the dialects of Northumbrian, Mercian and Kentish to name a few. However, most of what this book draws from is Old English as predominated by West Saxon.

Old English is very different from Middle and Modern English, insofar that it is often unrecognisable through pronunciations and letterings. Runes were a large form of literacy for early Anglo-Saxons, with the later Latin alphabet we all know coming in to reform the writing, perhaps in conjunction with the Christianisation of "proto-England."

A few letters in Old English come from the runic alphabet which have fallen into disuse (tragically, in my opinion). They are:

Ƿ ƿ; called a "Wynn;" pronounced "w."

Þ þ; called a "Thorn;" pronounced "th" which later replaced it.

Æ æ; called an "Ash;" pronounced often as "a."

Ð ð; called an "Eth" pronounced "th" yet softer than the Thorn.

— *Words and Phrases (in order of appearance)* —

— *Chapter 1* —

Eald enta geweorc — ancient work of giants
 A phrase pulled from the Anglo-Saxon poem *The Wanderer* which was used to describe the ruins left behind by the Romans.

Sceadugenga — nightwalker/shadowstalker/walker-in-the-night/shadow-goer
> The name given to Grendel in the poem Beowulf. It is the given name to the monster in this story.

Ic wille flæsc — I want flesh
> Grendel's desire for flesh or flæsc lain out, bloodthirsty as he is.

Lið — calm/stillness/rest
> The mental antonym to Grendel's flæsc, which signifies his bloodthirst. When this phrase appears, he has centred himself back to humanity.

Almigtig — almighty
> A phrase pulled directly from a stone in Newcastle about "Almighty God."

Muþa — mouth
> Referencing Tynemouth and the actual river itself.

nāne Scyldingas — no Scyldings
> Used synonymously with "warriors." Scyldings were a legendary tribe in Denmark whence hailed parts of the Anglo-Saxon ethnicity. They make much appearance in Beowulf.

Heord of flæsc — herd of flesh

Béordruncen — beer-drunk
> An invented "kenning," an Old English word made up of two or more.

Rætt — rat
> A rat appears, inciting bloodlust.

Nīðnihtlicgeweorc — work of night-like malice
> An invented compound comprised of *nīð* — "malice;" niht — "night;" -lic — "-like;" geweorc — "work." It is a modern mythopoetic creation meaning a thing shaped by the darkness of night, the shadows of sin and hatred. To quote Beowulf, "hateful to each was the breath of the other..." (lines 813-14 -

Michael Alexander translation).

drǣst — refuse/waste

Ciricragu — church-lichen or moss

bēoþ forþgānde wið sċeadwum — they are going forth with the shadows
A phrase referencing the shadowy nature of a narrow stairway.

tácn — symbol/token
The etymological ancestor to the word "token."

Sceadwum — shadows

Regnscur — rain-shower

se burg — the castle
A fascinating word related to the modern "borough" and still existent in the names of Germanic cities in Europe, their linguistic cousins.

Laþlic — hateful/loathsome
A phrase of spite in the eye's of Grendel.

Ða com of more under sceadumisthleoþum... me — then came from the moor beneath the shadow-mist-slopes... me
A phrase pulled straight from Beowulf, making the approach of Grendel to Heorot. This has been modified with *sceadu* inserted as well as *me* to change the perspective to Grendel and incorporate the shadows that are central to this story.

Ic bíte into flǣsc. Ic āþeġe. Ic ásúge þá steorfan, min hungor bierneð, gelíc eoten bealuhygdig. Heira drēora, þára drēora bestīemað mín tungan. Se ealdurnan ācwyle fyrst. He cennð bānum und pīnnessum, se cnafa āscað mé arian.
He onginð befleon swá sum nēatum butan sum adelsceaþe. He bierġð better ac hit is ne genyhtsum. Se þridda mann costað beorgan his orfeorme frēondum ac he mǣg ne be mé. Anbyrdnes? Gōd.
Ic feohte und he feohteð. Ic locie eat fyr his frēondum ac he is a mene wésa. Gōd. Regn gelic blōde, ge blod gelic regne. Regnscur. Blodscur. Ic undýde hine, bestīeme hine in him selfum.

Lið́s —
This passage is Grendel's feeding at the end, having spotted the three homeless men in the alcove. *Flǣsc* means "flesh," which Grendel bites *(bíte)* and devours *(āþeġe)*. *Ásúge* means "I suck out," here applied to *þā steorfan*, "the dying." Grendel's hunger burns *(bierneð)*, and he is likened to a *bealuhygdig eoten*, a "hateful-minded monster." *Drēora*, meaning "gore" or "dripping blood," is licked up by Grendel's tongue *(bestīemað mín tungan)*. The *ealdurnan*, the elder one dies first *(ācwyle fyrst)*. Another character *cennð bānum und pīnnessum*, "gives birth to bone and pain." The *cnafa* (the boy) pleads for mercy *(āscað mé arian)*, while the other flees *swá sum nēatum*, "like a beast," *butan sum adelsceaþe*, "without noble harm."

The third man tries to protect his *orfeorme frēondum*, "famished friends," but cannot. The creature reflects on *anbyrdnes*, endurance, experience, or perhaps the taste of it, and deems it *gōd*. The lines *regn gelic blōde, ge blōd gelic regne* (rain like blood, and blood like rain) cresendos the elemental violence, culminating in *regnscur, blodscur*, a rainshower, a bloodshower. Finally, the speaker *undýde hine*, "unmakes" or "opens him up," and *bestīeme hine in him selfum*, "drenches him in himself."

— Chapter 2 —

Ācyrsa þone Gēat — curse that Geat
The Geats were the tribe of Beowulf himself, the man who took Grendel's arm.

Sceadugenga bið þreatod — the nightwalker is threatened
The effect that the crucifix has on Grendel, himself being kindred to Cain.

Fals earm — false arm
The phantom limb left behind that still plagues Grendel.

Nā, ic eom gesewen — no, I am seen
Grendel's fears at being spotted by people in a car.

Endeþ hit nǣfre — does it never end

The road looks like it stretches on forever, but is this in reference to a literal road?

Holm — holly
> From where we get the word "holm oak" or "holly oak."

Bræþ — odour
> Even Grendel is not impervious to bad smells.

Wælhreowa — cruel slaughter
> An Anglo-Saxon curse of sorts.

Þæt bræmbor is ætstemped, afræst fram his wyrtrum — the bramble is trampled, torn up from its root
> An act of rage on unknowing foliage is something many could relate to.

Se sceadugenga slæpð — the nightwalker sleeps

Hwæt cymþ — what's happening

Ic eom gefunden! Hīe cōmon for mē — I am found! They are coming for me

— Chapter 3 —

Se sceadugenga gæð niðer on þæt heorðærn, his ham — The nightwalker goes down into the house-hall, his home
> Grendel goes down into the basement/cellar which the Doctor has fashioned into a home for him.

Þær nis nán līc — there is no corpse
> In consuming victims, Grendel leaves little-to-no evidence.

Hwæt is þis — what is this

Witung be Pinder — it's about Pinder

Hwæt gif folc cume sēcan hine — what if people seek him out

Ic þancie þē — I thank you

Ānlic þonne þū dēad eart — only once you are dead

Hwæt meinst þū — what do you mean

Þū sædest þæt sēo wīsdōm ealle þing mæge āsmēagan — you said science can answer all things

Ic eom mōdcræft — I am of mythology

— Chapter 4 —

Ic wille tōslītan hire flæsc. Ic wille hīe etan — I will tear her flesh apart. I will eat her

Hwæt is þes to — what is this for

Þes is gōd ingehygd — this is good invention

Sōþlīċe — indeed

Se sceadugenga grymet — the nightwalker grimaces

Hāl þū.
Ic bīte into flæsc. Hēo is swā wāc. Ic stice hīe. Ic stice hīe. Ic stice hīe. Ic stice hīe. Āgēan ond āgēan. Āgēan. Ic ontyne hīe ond tēo hyre flæsc tō mīnum mūðe. Hēo is mīn mete ond ic eom hyre hunta.
Hēo spæcð tō cīegean. Ic lecge mīnne mūþ ofer hyre ond bīte niþer. Hit is heard þæt ne bīte hyre hēafod of. Ic sceal brūcan þone earm. Ic slīce hīe. Ic stice hīe eft. Ic stice eft. Stice eft. Stice.
Þær is blōd ofer mé eall. Fæger. Hāt, wynsum, weleg blōd. Ēalā, hit is swā wundorlic. Hū lufie ic þæt bæðian onmanna blōde. Hit is swēte þing. For mīnne earm ic wille ofslean þūsend þūsendra manna ond wīfmannena. Ēalā, hū atēlic ond blīwlig ond winful ond fætt is þæs cildes lāþe blōd, ac hit is mīn tō genimenne eall swā same.
Lið̄s —

Grendel, in his second bloodlust, *stice* (I stab) and *tōslītan* (tears apart). The phrase *Ic bīte* into *flæsc*, "I bite into flesh" begins the feeding. The pronouns *hire* and *hīe* show us this is his first female victim in the story. *Ic stice hīe* (I stab her) is repeated, given that Grendel is using his new bionic arm to imitate human killings thanks to the Doctor.

Āgēan ond āgēan (again and again) Grendel attacks her. He continues: (*ontyne hīe ond tēo hyre flæsc tō mīnum mūðe*) "I tear her apart and pull her flesh to my mouth."

The victim attempts to cry out (*hēo spæcð tō cīegean*) but is silenced by Grendel instead, *Ic lecge mīnne mūþ ofer hyre ond bīte niþer* (I lay my mouth over hers and bite down). Grendel has control and does not: *þæt ne bīte hyre hēafod of* (It is hard so I do not bite her head off). He must pretend to kill as a human.

Blood (*blōd*) is *fæger, hāt, wynsum*, and *weleg*, "fair," "hot," "pleasing," and "rich." Grendel bathes in *manna blōde* ("manblood").

Grendel wants to slay *þūsend þūsendra manna ond wīfmannena* (thousands and thousands of men and women). *Atēlic ond blīwlig ond winful ond fætt* (terrible and bitter and intoxicating and fat) is the hateful blood of the victim, Grendel's wonting and wanting.

— Chapter 5 —

Ic ete þæt rottene flæsc. Hit smæcð yfel. Ic hæbbe to fela deaðlicra līchaman geetan. Þæt flæsc is swilce yfel wæter. Hit is yfel þære tunge. Hit is yfel þam steortan. Ic ete and asende þone līc awęg. Hī węncað þæt rætan þæt flæsc geęton —

Grendel eats *rottene flæsc*, "rotten flesh." *Hit smæcð yfel*, "It tastes evil" as it is an already dead body. He has eaten to *fela deaðlicra līchaman*, "too many deadly bodies."

The flesh is *swilce yfel wæter*, "like evil water," and *yfel þære tunge*, "evil to the tongue," *yfel þam steortan*, "evil to the taste buds palate."

He *ete and asende þone līc awęg*, "eats and sends the corpse away," to completion. *Hī węncað þæt rætan þæt flæsc geęton*, "They think the rats ate the flesh." The people do not know he dwells beneath.

Is þis palentse — is this a palace
>   Grendel still cannot always tell the difference. He is more ignorant a few hundred years ago.

Þa sceadugas — the shadows

Ic grip þone lytlan cniht. I stinga mine clawu into his muð, and he ne mæg sceamian. His eagan widuþ, þæt ic him eallunga forþan to slægenne, and drincþ his blode. Eala, hu swete and frisce is his flæsc! Eala, hu wundorful! Hu mære! Swa swiðe deor is feor þæt ic hit gemet in þa stræte of Paris.
Ic hæbbe þa lænan dæl to læte —
>   *Ic grip þone lytlan cniht,* "I grasp the little boy." *Ic stinga mine clawu into his muð,* "I stab my claw into his mouth" and he *ne mæg sceamian,* "he cannot scream." His eyes are wide, *his eagan widuþ* and Grendel, *þæt ic him eallunga forþan to slægenne,* "utterly kills him" to *drincþ his blode,* "drink his blood." *Eala, hu swete and frisce is his flæsc! Eala, hu wundorful! Hu mære!* is rejoicing, "how sweet and fresh is flesh," "how wonderful," "how excellent." So very precious is it that I found it in the streets of Paris, *swa swiðe deor is feor þæt ic hit gemet in þa stræte of Paris.*
>   *Ic hæbbe þa lænan dæl to læte,* "I give a piece of myself to him."

bærnþ — burns

Wyrd — fate/destiny
>   This word evolved to "weird" but it's original meaning is more poetic.

God — God

Hælend — saviour

Metod — lord

Wealdend — "ruler"

Mæg hē mē geseon — can he see me
Grendel thinks this as he sees the mighty church, thinking of God.

Þa legu sind fordigde. Bita be bita hi beoð fornumene oð þæt hi fyndað fostor. Nis micel belifen, ac hit is genoh for þa niht, and se sunne cymð sona —

The legs are brought down. Bit by bit they are taken away until they find shelter. Not much is left, but it is enough for the night, and the sun comes soon

— Chapter 6 —

anhaga — solitary one/lone one

eardstappa — earth-stepper

hāl, frēond — hello friend
Grendel communes with a crow, a fellow flesh-eater in vain.

His dagoras brecað.
Ic gripige his earm and rippe hit of mid minum tēoth. Ic et hit onforan him, þonne he wāt, to wērdan his mōd. Hē spītt blod. Ic spitte his agen blod on him. Ic et hine fram fōt to healf. Hē hlypð eallunga þæt ic rīce his byrst. Hē smēlt gōd. Hē smēlt of wīn hē drincþ and blod þæt ic drinc. Hit is god mete. Soldēra ēac smēlt gōd. Ic rippe his cīep of to forlēosan mine mete. Ic et þæt læstan of him. Hit is god mete —

His dagoras brecað means "his days are numbered." Grendel rips off the man's arm with his teeth, *Ic gripige his earm and rippe hit of mid minum tēoth*. Grendel eats "onforan him," before him, showing his attack to the victim *to wērdan his mōd*, "to unmake his spirit." *Hē spītt blod. Ic spitte his agen blod on him,* is the splitting of blood onto one another until *Ic et hine fram fōt to healf*, "I eat him from bottom to top.' *Hē hlypð eallunga þæt ic rīce his byrst,* is the victim "jerking" violently in death. He smells good, *hē smēlt gōd*, and *of wīn hē drincþ and blod þæt ic drinc,* "of wine he drank through the blood I drink." Hit is god mete, is "it is good meat." *Ic rippe his cīep of to forlēosan mine mete* is "I tear off his cheek to claim my meat."

— Chapter 7 —

wǣtan — pus

blōd — blood

ādle — disease

untrumnes — weakness

lēgesēocnes — pestilence

plege — plague

mānseocnes — sickness

wælcyme — incoming slaughter

Hē is sēoc — he is sick

Mid ānum earmum ic his swūran genime — I seize his neck with one hand

Ic þrēate, and his hēafod sprincð of. Hē bersteð swā fūl frēolīc wæstm, and sēa dēaðes ādl mid him ūtgæð. Ic ne mæg geswīcan. Ic þearf etan. Ānlic hit mē þurhteōn þæt ic swelte. Ic slite mid mīnum tōþum þǣre stōwe þǣr his hēafod ǣr wæs, and ic drince. Ic hæbbe nān oþer weġ, nān geweald.
Hit is yfel mēte —

Ic þrēate, and his hēafod sprincð of, is "ripping his head off" and he bersteð swā fūl frēolīc wæstm, and sēa dēaðes ādl mid him ūtgæð, "ruptures like a foul, overripe fruit, and the sickness of death flows out with him" which is due to the Black Plague infesting the corpse which he eats. Despite this, Grendel mæg geswīcan, "cannot stop" as he þearf etan, "must eat. Only starvation would kill him, ānlic hit mē þurhteōn þæt ic swelte.

Ic slite mid mīnum tōþum þǣre stōwe þǣr his hēafod ǣr wæs, he "tears with his teeth at the place where a head once was," and drinks. Ic hæbbe nān oþer weġ, nān geweald, "I have no other way, no control.

Hit is yfel mēte, "it is awful meat."

Egesa! Egesa! Mōdor, hwǣr eart þū — Terror! Terror! Mother, where are you?

The first part of this story where Grendel acknowledges his mother's existence (or previous existence) in an emotional fashion.

Ic wille on life wunian — I wish to live

— Chapter 8 —

fenhleoðu — marsh-slopes
    The marshy slopes of Grendel's home - we have reached the place of Beowulf's occurrence.

Þes hāl — be well

Ic gretie þé — I greet you

Hū ys þīn earm — how is your arm

Ænglisc — English

Ic eom — I am

Englaland — England/Land of the Angles
    The old and early name for England which the Vikings came to later use.

Far þider — go there

Caines cyn — kindred of Cain

Seolfor — silver

Ryn — run

— Chapter 9 —

Mīn earm — my arm

— *Chapter 10* —

ġeþōht — relfection/reason

Hungor — hunger

Blōdlust — bloodlust

Ānnes — loneliness

Wœclic — loathsomeness

Frēondscipe — friendship

Eom ic brōþor — I am a brother?

ABOUT THE AUTHOR

Frederick Atkinson is a writer and literary influencer focusing on the "canon" as well as the ebb and flow of myth, language, history and much more. Whilst he discusses the so-called classics, his true love is of the dark and eldritch underbelly of literature. He adores the Greco-Roman writings and mythos, but truly has a heart for Anglo-Saxon and wider Germanic poetry. He prefers Woden to Zeus and elves to nymphs.

Frederick has a BA in English Literature and a subsequent MA in Creative Writing from Newcastle University, graduating in December of 2024. Born in 2001, he has been writing all his life, and this is the first of his works to be put to the light of publication - he hopes the shadows of this eerie, challenging piece show well in such a glow.

Printed in Dunstable, United Kingdom